# DEREK S. WRUTH

# SOLACE RISES

BOOKSIDE Press

Copyright © 2024 by Derek S. Wruth

ISBN: 978-1-77883-346-5 (Paperback)

978-1-77883-347-2 (Hardback)

978-1-77883-348-9 (E-book)

All rights reserved. No part of this publication may be reproduced, distributed, or transmitted in any form or by any means, including photocopying, recording, or other electronic or mechanical methods, without the prior written permission of the publisher, except in the case brief quotations embodied in critical reviews and other noncommercial uses permitted by copyright law.

The views expressed in this book are solely those of the author and do not necessarily reflect the views of the publisher, and the publisher hereby disclaims any responsibility for them. Some names and identifying details in this book have been changed to protect the privacy of individuals.

BookSide Press
877-741-8091
www.booksidepress.com
orders@booksidepress.com

# Contents

Chapter One ............................................................................. 7
Chapter Two ............................................................................ 13
Chapter Three ......................................................................... 19
Chapter Four ........................................................................... 24
Chapter Five ............................................................................ 28
Chapter Six .............................................................................. 35
Chapter Seven ........................................................................ 46
Chapter Eight .......................................................................... 52
Chapter Nine ........................................................................... 58
Chapter Ten ............................................................................. 63
Chapter Eleven ....................................................................... 68
Chapter Twelve ....................................................................... 74
Chapter Thirteen .................................................................... 79
Chapter Fourteen ................................................................... 83
Chapter Fifteen ....................................................................... 88
Chapter Sixteen ...................................................................... 95
Chapter Seventeen .............................................................. 100
Chapter Eighteen ................................................................. 106
Chapter Nineteen ................................................................. 112
Chapter Twenty .................................................................... 119
Chapter Twenty-One ........................................................... 123
Chapter Twenty-Two ........................................................... 130
Chapter Twenty-Three ........................................................ 135
Chapter Twenty-Four .......................................................... 140
Chapter Twenty-Five ........................................................... 144
Chapter Twenty-Six ............................................................. 151

## Dedication:

For Leaton and Randy, because of you two I will always aspire to be a better man.

# Chapter One

A sign.
Trees.
Another sign.
More trees.
Hey a building, that was a nice change of pace.

It had been nearly ten hours of more or less the same scenery, trees and road signs, and it was beginning to become slightly unbearable. Where were they going? What was happening?

They were in the middle of enjoying a nice evening supper when Dad got the phone call. Eiri was not sure who was on the other end but whoever it was sure had said something that his Dad didn't particularly want to nor care to hear. When the conversation had come to an abrupt end, all that Mom and Eiri were told was that they were to pack a few things and they were going on what Dad had called an "interim road-trip". They had been rubber on pavement ever since, with limited bathroom breaks.

Eiri watched through the back window as plains terraformed into trees and then slowly into mountain passes and curvy mountain roads. The sun had gone under the horizon and he watched the moon make her nightly walk across the skies from east to west, she hung just off center more to the west now.

Every few minutes or so Eiri would watch Mom reach over and grab Dad's arm. It wouldn't have appeared as much to anyone else who was to witness such a gesture but to someone who knew the two, namely he, Eiri knew what that small movement suggested.

"We're going to be okay hun."

The crooked smile Dad gave back to her each time she did it also had its own set of wordless notion.

"I know."

The level of understanding between the two had always been tangible to him and Eiri had to imagine everyone else who saw them in a room together could also say the same. Their connection was pretty palpable. They could hold full conversations using strictly eye movement and body language. It was beautiful and even from a young age he knew that wherever he ended up, Eiri would strive to find such beauty in a connection as these two had found perfectly within each other.

"You doing alright back there kiddo?"

"Yes Mom. I'm good. Are we going to stop soon? I have to use the bathroom."

"Can we stop for a bit Hugh?'

Dad sat in silence, perhaps pondering the pros and cons of such a demand.

"I believe I saw a campsite sign a little ways back so we should be coming up on the place soon. I could use a good stretch for my legs. I think stopping would be a grand idea son."

The sound of gravel crunching under tires was a rather nice adjustment from the quietness of the highway. The air felt heavier as soon as the family station wagon turned off the pavement.

Then the pain hit Eiri in the stomach and it spread through his arms and down his spine.

"You okay Eir," his mom asked as soon as it began to happen. The motherly instincts must have kicked in because Eiri hadn't said a word or uttered a sound.

"I'm okay. I just feel weird."

"We'll be stopping soon honey. Here. Drink some water."

The sight of an old building came within view of the headlights and signalled a restroom had come along to save the day.

Eiri couldn't shake the feeling building in his gut.

"Okay Eir you get to hold the flashlight until we get inside. How's that sound?'

"That sounds good Dad."

The cool night air chilled Eiri instantly as he opened the door to step outside.

"Dad do you feel that?"

"What do you mean son?"

Eiri tried to find the words to describe what he felt as they walked up to that outhouse. Even now he couldn't quite explain what he was feeling. It just didn't feel right. He did remember though that as they got closer to the outhouse that two large shadows standing like sentinels on either side of the place began to move and Eiri did think that was odd. He couldn't picture it as clearly now so he must have thought it was a bush or something at the time.

"I dunno I just feel…."

Eiri never got to finish that sentence when they attacked. It all happened so fast.

A large thud noise broke the silence. The sound of Dads muffled yell. Then the liquid hit Eiri's face and he lost control.

A strange burning sensation ran down his spine, it radiated from his stomach and shot along both his arms. Eiri remembered his fists began to hurt and then the bright lights came. That's when everything went black. Everything went quiet. It all was so quiet.

"Well I dislike having to stop you there sir but I'm afraid I have to for today. The hour's up now but we'll do same time next week then?"

The sudden voice shook Eiri from his mind and for a moment he had forgotten where he was.

"No problem doc. I'm looking forward to it."

"Just make an appointment with Mary on the way out. Talk to you soon my friend," the doc replied, already shuffling through papers which Eiri imagined was in regards to the next patient. He couldn't imagine how many "broken" people the guy had to sit down with each day, wouldn't blame the guy if he were a closet drinker.

On his way out, after scheduling an appointment with the lovely brunette haired receptionist known as Mary, Eiri felt something change in the air and it gave him chills.

"Hey man I believe you dropped this."

Eiri turned around to see where the voice came from and he saw a man running up to him holding a card.

He took the card from him and thanked him for his courtesy. The stranger seemed anxious but Eiri didn't blame him. After all, it was a therapist's office. The places weren't known for their social appeal.

The scar above the man's left eye stood out to Eiri. God whatever happened sure was close to taking his eye with it.

Eiri made his way down the stairs, he skipped the elevator because the doc stated he should exercise more to help quell his moods, and the closer he got to the bottom the more relaxed he felt. Eiri's legs feeling like jelly mostly took the attention off his mind to the fact he felt he was nearly dying, though it also reminded him that he should go for a run more often. The heavy tension that he had picked up slowly faded away from him. The outside air also helped him feel better and despite all the cars on the street, the air felt clean.

On his way home Eiri stopped at a small deli on the corner just down from his apartment and ordered a sub and a coke. He almost decided to eat there and enjoy the day but then he realised how busy it was and he figured against that, he'd rather sit alone at home. Too many people had him feeling more anxious than relaxed.

When Eiri arrived back at home he glanced at the table. Two plates set for a meal. He almost cleared it and ate there but changed his mind and settled for the couch in front of the television instead.

He flipped the news on and sat down to enjoy his ham sandwich with lettuce.

Headline after headline of tragedy and unfortunate events was all that seemed to play nowadays. Why Eiri kept watching each day he didn't know and despite how many times he told myself it wasn't a good idea, he went against it and watched it anyway.

Train derailing, a warehouse fire which killed two and injured several others, including a fireman, the anniversary of a larger more devastating warehouse fire, which ended up claiming the lives of two firefighters, a man and a woman. It all seemed so negative. Where was the news of the miracle babies born? Or the animals that weren't on the endangered species list anymore?

It was so quiet in here, a tranquil sanctuary that bereft Eiri of the typical noise of the city surrounding him. Though if he stayed still he could hear there was the buzzing of a fan running off in his bedroom, the leaky faucet above the sink in the kitchen, maybe it wasn't too quiet. The steady pulse of electrical devices plugged-in in their various places around the apartment made his head throb, Eiri thought he should put on some music. Maybe that would help.

A light melody of something with a guitar would do it, after all Eiri wasn't picky. A slow melody came over the small speaker that the stereo had built in. Perfect. Eiri then set his sights on the book he was attempting to read, Strangers by Dean Koontz. It was one of his favorites and this would be his tenth time reading it. Now normally his attention would be hooked and page after page he would lose himself in it, strung along through suspense and bewilderment, but lately he couldn't focus. On anything.

11:00pm.

That was the time Eiri finally looked at the clock. He had done absolutely nothing productive today since his meeting this morning. Eiri called them meetings because it made him feel better about himself, internally you know.

Eiri felt funny. Perhaps because he hadn't really eaten today, outside of the sub and coke earlier on and he was far too tired to make something. His bed sounded a lot more enticing.

The bathroom mirror stuck again when he went to grab his pills out of it. Stupid thing never opened smoothly anymore. Dam this apartment. It was always messing with him in some way.

A loud bang woke Eiri from his sleep. Like something falling loudly on the floor.

1:33am.

Without even putting thought into it he found himself on his feet holding the .45 from under his pillow and inching slowly towards his bedroom door. Whoever was out there sure better be ready for a fight.

He could hear quiet movement. The odd thud sounded out echoing off the empty walls.

Eiri inched closer towards his bedroom door and realised it hung slightly ajar. He knew he closed it before he laid down, he always did.

Closer.

Slower.

Careful.

He reached for the doorknob.

Eiri gripped his gun even tighter.

The sounds outside had stopped.

He held the handle, steadying his breathing.

Then his door flew open from the other side.

# Chapter Two

Evelyn Towne was never one for hanging out at the mall to shop for hours simply because that was the thing women loved to do. No Evelyn would much rather live outside the city limits and read books under the afternoon sun while she waited for her coffee to brew, she tried the whole green tea trend once because of something she read on the internet but it never seemed to give her the buzz that copious amounts of caffeine did, after all she was a novelist and a night owl. This all in turn is precisely why when she had landed the small acreage outside the city she had realised one thing, Evelyn Towne was happy.

The three bedroom house came relatively cheap and on a writer's salary this had worked perfect for her and her collie named Candy. She had picked up Candy when she was a small pup from an animal shelter in the city and through a lot of love and affection she had trained the dog rather well. Her best friend, a cup of coffee and a good book was all Evelyn needed to get through the day.

She had been stuck on the new book she was writing. Just a good case of writer's block to stop the aspiring artist dead in her tracks after successfully writing and publishing her third book. She had heard of this but fortunately she had never before dealt with it personally. Typically when she wanted to write to put food on the table the words just flowed onto paper in the most beautiful of ways. It came to Evelyn at a young age that this was what she wanted to do. Write stories. She absolutely loved a good book and despite the advancement of technology filling her with fear she wouldn't sell any copies, she had proven herself wrong and luckily made a decent living writing hardcover novels.

At half past three on Saturday, Evelyn got the phone call that forever changed her life.

"Mom and dad have been in an accident. They're in emergency right now."

"I'm on my way," was all Evelyn could say after hearing the news, hurriedly grabbing her keys and telling Candy she would be back.

"Evelyn. You better hurry."

At 9:00pm that same Saturday Evelyn kissed her mom and her dad for the last time. There was nothing the doctors hadn't tried and with all the progress in medicine and healthcare they couldn't save Evelyn's beloved parents. She sat in the waiting room with her older sister and younger brother for nearly six hours as the medical team tried to stabilize her parents. The truck that had hit them and pushed them off a steep embankment was driven by a young teenager who decided it was okay to operate a motorized vehicle after six beers. He had been killed in the accident almost instantly. And while Evelyn imagined her parents clinging to life, fighting with all they had to see their children one more time promising each other they couldn't go, they left. No goodbye. No "I love you" or "look after your brother", just silence. The teen had taken them.

After sitting with her siblings and deciding they'd meet up within the next few days to go over things, Evelyn headed home. Blurry eyed and heavy hearted.

She stopped for something to drink on the way home and picked up some vodka to help her sleep tonight. She hoped it would help stop the anger building in her gut. The resentment she felt for that bloody teenager, who couldn't even say sorry.

It was nearly midnight that Saturday when Evelyn came around the bend before the bridge. A slow rain had picked up and this made the roads a little slippery.

She saw the car coming up and as soon as their lights met her eyes, her gut began to hurt.

She had been trying to set her windshield wipers to a good speed to deal with the water droplets building on her window when out of the ditch a deer ran out.

Evelyn slammed her brakes and this caused her to slide a little to the left into the oncoming lane.

The deer jumped almost as if to try and jump over her small car.

The vehicle she just met slammed on their brakes and tried swerving right, wherein they must have seen the deer and then swerved left instead, towards Evelyn.

The burning began in her gut and went down both arms and for whatever reason Evelyn stuck her hand out forward.

The car almost hit into her when suddenly it went onto its' passenger side and slid like a toboggan past her car, missing her by inches.

The deer in mid-air shot violently into the trees on Evelyn's left side, breaking branches and rag dolling to the ground.

Through her rear-view mirror Evelyn watched as the car that almost hit her teetered for a bit, still with the passenger side down on the ground, after skidding to a slow stop then toppled onto its' roof.

Evelyn and her car remained unharmed, just sitting there.

She looked down at her hands. They were stinging, the right one especially.

What the hell was that Evelyn thought to herself?

Then Evelyn got out and ran to the other car to help whoever was in there.

It was 12:30am on an early Sunday morning.

The next afternoon Evelyn woke up with one hell of a headache and a sore back. She went for the phone and called the hospital, hoping to hear news on Todd. That was the other driver she had met last night. Poor Todd was unconscious the entire time and even after the ambulance showed up to take him in.

"I'm sorry Miss Towne but if you aren't family we aren't at liberty to say how he is doing."

"Can I come in and see him than?"

"Someone might come to you," the voice added then hung up.

A knock at the door startled Evelyn.

"Some guard dog you are Candy. You didn't even let me know someone was here."

She went and answered the door and as she passed a window she saw the cop car sitting in her driveway. Why was a policeman here? She had answered their questions last night.

"May I come in," the young cop asked after she opened the door.

"Sure, yeah, uhh don't mind the mess. Been a rough weekend officer," Evelyn said to him.

"I can imagine ma'am. It's no problem."

"Care for a hot drink or anything officer," she asked as they sat at her kitchen table.

"No ma'am that's quite alright. I shouldn't be here long. Just have a few more questions to ask you and I'll be on my way."

The officer followed Evelyn into the door and toward the kitchen area; he scanned his head about as he walked behind her. Searching and looking Evelyn suspected, she thought he looked awfully short to be a cop.

"Alright, so what do you want to know sir," she replied.

The young cop took off his hat and adjusted how he was sitting, the name on his uniform read Constable Smith.

"Mr. Johnson passed away a few hours after you left the hospital. He never regained consciousness Evelyn. I'm sorry to have to tell you this way but being as you were there we need to fully understand just what happened. "

She heard him. She knew Constable Smith was there. Even with all that was going on at that moment, Evelyn Towne couldn't help but break down into tears.

"I know this can't be easy Miss Towne and I'm sorry to have to do this, in such a manner. Believe me I know this. But this is what we have to do now," Smith said to her.

"I don't know," Evelyn answered through tears.

"There was the deer and then he must have lost control…" she began to explain when Constable Smith stopped her short.

"We found the deer. It was mangled. We think an animal got to it before we did. There wasn't much left of it and after further examination on Mr. Johnson. There's just something that doesn't add up. We're just trying to understand ma'am."

"What do you mean," she asked.

"The left side of Mr. Johnsons' skull was damaged. His driver window is smashed and his car is dented all the way down from end to end."

"I told you he slid on the side though. I saw his car topple onto the roof."

"Oh I don't doubt that at all, there's corresponding damage to support that, but that was on the passenger side. Your driver side is fine, meaning he never hit you. So what hit him so hard on his drivers' side that it killed him," he asked.

Evelyn looked down at her hand, then to Constable Smith, then to Candy. She thought for a minute on telling him what she did but then considered how he would take it.

"I don't know sir," she answered instead.

"Yeah it's rather odd. Well ma'am thank you for your time. If we need to contact you we'll be in touch. Oh and in case you remember anything," he said as he handed her a card.

"Give us a call. Take care now," the young man added as he stood to leave.

"Oh and Evelyn, stay close to home."

"Yes sir," she replied.

As the cruiser pulled away down her road, Evelyn broke down onto her kitchen floor. She was full of pain and confusion. Whatever the hell was in the air this weekend she hoped to hell that it would just go away, somewhere far away. She screamed to the sky. To whoever the hell was listening up there. Questioning just what she did so bad to deserve any of this. The thoughts plagued her mind.

Had she killed Todd Johnson with whatever had potentially saved her life that night?

She stared at her hands, almost fearful of them. What had she done?

Who the hell could she tell? The questions went on and on in her mind and she honestly had no idea what she was supposed to do now. Did they know? What was she? She had to know.

Evelyn stormed out her back door into her backyard and headed for the nearby trees. She had to think and the trees would help her. That was her spot after all, in the trees and near the creek, tucked away from the rest of the world, away from death and hurt and pain…away from her.

"Come along Candy, follow mom."

Candy barked a small bark in agreement and pranced behind Evelyn as they walked to the woods.

"I'm glad you're with me Candy. You keep me sane girl."

Candy barked again.

"Good puppy."

# Chapter Three

"You have got to cut that shit out I am telling yous, it'll kill you."

Benjamin Ryder was leaning against his truck just after work and as he cracked a cold beer, he heard those ever inspirational words from his co-worker and friend, however thin that word may be, Jeremy.

"What doesn't kill you nowadays," Ben shot back, he wasn't in the mood for the banter today.

"Well I have to give you that, you got a point," Jeremy answered.

"Get in the truck Jer. Let's get the hell out of here."

As they drove into town from the work site they talked about the long day and how bad the boss was at his job. This seemed to be the daily conversation following a ten hour day chopping trees and piling deadfall. No matter how the day, good or bad, they were never short of things to complain about on the way to their hotel. Funny that this actually occurred to Ben in his head but he didn't ever plan on doing something about it, this was just how it was.

"Well should we grab some pizza or something? I'm famished," Ben asked his passenger.

"Yeah that sounds better than dam overcooked noodles again man."

They pulled into a pizza joint and ordered a large pepperoni and a ham and pineapple. The place offered a two for one deal so they couldn't pass up grabbing the extra, though it would probably sit out and remain not eaten in their hotel room.

The town they were in didn't have much for businesses. Ben saw a gas station slash convenience store, a liquor store and a bar hotel looking building. The lovely little pit of isolation also came with the typical residential area for the locals of course and from a distance Ben thought he could see a trailer park. Typical small town in Alberta, at least it had a couple places to buy cheap beer.

After the pizza was ready they headed back to the hotel. The company they worked for put them up here and the room quality was definitely something to be questioned but hell the place wasn't too bad, I mean they took what they could, this could have been worse Ben supposed. Least the place had a roof.

"Hey I'm going to grab a shower and I'll pop back in. Think I'll have one of those cold ones with you," Jeremy said as they got to the upper level of the hotel and approached their rooms.

"For sure man, I'll have one waiting."

Dam Ben thought, he should have bought more.

As he walked into his room Ben threw his bag onto the floor beside the bed. What a long dam day he thought as he peeled off his steel-toed boots and pulled back his button up shirt. The soreness sat in his shoulders today, whereas most days it settled into his lower back.

He begun to think a cool shower would be great as well, so he threw the beer in the mini-fridge, placed the pizza on the table and proceeded to go to the small bathroom.

The water ran over him and he felt his muscles tense. Maybe, he thought to himself, the cold shower after a workout relaxes your muscles myth was true, but the hell he was going to try though. He'd been cold the majority of the day, he'd be damned to be cold in a controlled environment any more than need be today.

Following his shower Ben sat on his small couch and ate pizza. He had started his sixth beer when Jeremy showed up, eager to converse.

"So man I think tomorrow I'm going to do it. I am going to tell him exactly what is on my mind."

Ben looked at his friend, "you say that at least three times a week. It's been almost four months now. I'm no good at probabilities or numbers but there's a good chance you won't."

"To hell with you man," Jeremy replied, sounding almost shocked at Ben's response of quick wit.

"You just know if I did that he'd promote me or something. You relish the fact when I don't actually do it you selfish prick," Jeremy said back to Ben, laughing as he did.

"You know me too well Jerrbear, because you my friend are a genius," Ben sarcastically answered.

The two spent the next couple hours talking and bullshitting as most friends do while consuming barley soup. They spoke on the old days, reminiscing and carrying on about the ones that got away, who they hated in high school, how they hoped half those pricks peaked in junior high and which teachers were the worst. The two had spent many nights working together but rarely did they unwind and talk the talk. Mostly they kept with work but tonight it caught up. They both needed the time to sit and just talk. There was something oddly pleasant about having a good friend and a cold drink.

Ben and Jeremy had grown up together. A small one horse kind of town was where they called home and there really wasn't much to the place. About 1400 people lived there, although it may have grown now, as most towns do in time. The size of the place allowed for a more homegrown feel though and was definitely less hectic than any city you could stop in. Farming and the oilfield were the backbone to the place and that's just what you did, at least you had a choice.

After school had ended the two never even tried to go for further education. That just wasn't something either wanted, they were both raised for hard work though and fortunately they had landed a job in the forest industry within the same company. Jeremy had been married but after too many nights away from home that had come to a sudden end. She took the house and his crossover but in many ways he never seemed too broken hearted over the fact. He maintained that he saw it coming; he always said it was hard to keep a relationship when you're gone two thirds of the year. Guess he was right.

Benjamin himself had never been married; he'd never been with someone for over three months. Whatever the case was, he just wasn't lucky in the love department, which suited him just fine. He kept busy with work and when he wasn't working he enjoyed his beer and his television.

At around 2:30am that Friday night Jeremy finished his last beer and decided he had better go try the sleep thing, seeing as how he had a lot to say tomorrow to a certain higher up.

"I'm telling you, it's going to happen," Jeremy kept saying as he stumbled for the door.

"Fuck Wilkinson, he's no better off than we are, he just knows the right people."

Ben ended up closing the door on his friend, knowing that if he didn't that he would have to listen to more of the same Wilkinson this, Wilkinson that conversation and he had enough of that for one night.

The last time he glanced at the clock it was nearing 3:00am. Then sleep took him. Ben stood on a hill. The air around him was filled with thick smoke and smelled of burning…something that he couldn't quite pinpoint. There was a loud groaning noise, metallic-like and deep, off in the distance. A figure beside him walked up and grabbed his shoulder.

"Crazy isn't it," the man said.

"We have to find him now; he'll know what to do. We have to find him."

The man looked at him and right away Ben saw the scar above his left eye. It was glowing.

Ben moved his mouth but no words came out, no sounds came from him.

Then everything shifted and Ben felt the hair on his body raise up. From up above somewhere, a man floated down beside them. Two more people followed him. The first of the three then looked at Ben. His arms were glowing.

"Wake up."

The alarm on his bedside table woke him cold from his slumber.

"What the hell," Ben said as he hit his dismiss button.

I'm never drinking again he thought quietly to himself, never again.

The knock at his door a half hour later was the telltale sign that it was time to get at er. It was time to go cut some trees and score some earth and although Ben didn't particularly agree with the work they were doing: it did put clothes on his back and food in his stomach. That's what mattered.

"Another day another dollar Benny. Aren't ya excited?"

"I can't believe my luck."

# Chapter Four

Eiri sat in the waiting room, waiting to talk to the doc again. Wondering just how exactly the man would delve into his mind today. What words he could say that would unlock the traumatic experiences from Eiris' past and help him build a better more stable future?

Would he interpret the dream he had a week ago? The freaky one about the break in at his apartment, he wondered would he make sense of it and how real it felt. Could he tell Eiri why he had awakened covered in sweat and screaming following said dream? Eiri didn't know the answers but he highly doubted the doctor did either.

Eiri was hoping that today would not be a full meeting though. The doc himself had a meeting, and Eiri wondered if he had it as code for his own therapy. What Eiri wouldn't give to be a fly on the wall for that.

"Mr. Stephens," said a soft voice from behind the desk, "you can go in now."

"Thanks Mary," he replied back with a half-smile.

"Good morning Eiri," the man in the suit said on the better side of a clipboard.

"How are you today? How was the last week for you?"

"More or less the same," Eiri said back, not wanting to be sitting in the hot seat at all this week.

"I had a dream."

"Hmm. Tell me about this dream," the doctor inquisitively insisted.

"It was at my apartment. There was a break in and I killed the guy doing it," I told him.

"Interesting indeed but yet somehow I feel you have more to say about it."

The guy was good. That wasn't the weird part of his dream at all; the odd part was how Eiri killed the guy. Eiri had a gun but instead of using it he had instead in some way managed to fry the guy using only his hands. It was pretty messed up. But it felt familiar if that made any sense.

"Have you ever seen a Star Wars movie where the Emperor shoots lightning out of his hands," Eiri asked the doc hoping that he was a fan of good movies so he could make some comparison to what exactly he saw happen in his dream.

"No I don't believe I have. Why do you ask?"

"Okay well because uhh....well I shot the guy. With my bare hands...with like electricity...I think. If you can understand what I mean," Eiri awkwardly tried to explain.

"You mean to say you shocked a man in your dream using your hands?"

"Yes. Exactly," Eiri said back in relief seeing that he knew what he meant.

"And this happened at your apartment after the man attempted to break in and we are to assume steal something. Am I correct in saying that?"

"Yes sir. Spot on."

"Okay well. I don't think how you killed the man holds any kind of special meaning seeing as how you've seen this done in a movie. But I think the fact that it was about an attempted break in at your place where you are meant to feel safe is a significant breakthrough."

"I'm sorry? What do you mean by that?"

"Well. Dreams are important when read into correctly. The mind typically manifests in dreams as its current state as a house, or a lake. Choppy unsettled water could mean you have a lot on your mind, same goes for a cluttered house; whereas tranquil water or a tidy house would mean the opposite, a sense of serenity in your mind. See what I mean? It embodies as something that we can physically see in a dream. In this case I believe you feel threatened from someone or something attacking your mind. Subconsciously I believe you felt that this invasion into your home was an attempt to hurt you."

Eiri looked at the doc in bewilderment and at that moment he wanted to argue. To tell him he was wrong, to mention that when he was little something happened that this was connected to and how Eiri knew that, he didn't understand but it sure as hell wasn't anything related to what he was getting at.

"Okay. So how do we go about finding what that is then doc," is what Eiri asked instead.

"Well I think. You need to start journaling and dream journaling too. Write down everything. In the waking hours and after you wake up from sleeping. Try to remember your dreams and write them down. Document your thoughts. And bring it to me next week and we'll go from there. Okay?"

"Whatever you think will work doc," I answered. Knowing I wasn't going to do that at all.

The two talked for a little while longer and when Eiri thought he was about to explode with all the care bear crap the doc said the magic words.

"So Mr. Stephens same time next week then? Tell Mary on your way out and take care," he said back, already going through more papers.

"Thanks doc, I guess until next time. See ya."

Eiri did as he was told and grabbed an appointment card on the way out, thanked Mary the receptionist and headed for the stairs.

He couldn't believe the crock of shit that man just told me. Eiri thought he was having a serious breakthrough and then the doc flipped it into complete nonsense. Un-flipping-believable. There was no way in hell Eiri was coming back next week. No dam way.

The elevator ding echoed in the hall as Eiri closed in on the stairs and as he turned the corner he happened to see the man who had returned his appointment card he had dropped last week, while entering the doctors' office.

"Guy's a fucking liar," Eiri almost yelled to the man," don't waste your time."

The feeling was back and Eiri hadn't realised it had come back until it almost made him hurl. His arms began to tingle and the lights in the stairwell began to flicker.

What the heck was this all about?

After a few seconds it passed and Eiri felt alright again.

What the hell was wrong with him?

The lights returned to the stairwell and so he continued the way down.

And down. And down.

As he stepped outside into the blinding sunlight he found comfort in the fact that he didn't feel like laying down instantaneously. Eiri had made a point of taking a morning walk each day, maybe he wouldn't journal but he did entertain the thought of having an outlet to release some excess energy. Also the lady who made coffee down the street had very pretty eyes.

# Chapter Five

It had been over a week since the accidents and Evelyn no longer felt in control of her own life. Mr. Johnsons' family had been harassing her thus resulting in a constant presence from the local police. Following Evelyn and calling her and hounding her. She just wanted it to go back to the way it was a week ago. This had been a nightmare and she couldn't help but feel that her solitude had been ripped away from her.

She had only been to town a handful of times the last week and only to grab food and to go to a library to gather books. She had begun reading up on some new things she was interested in. A week ago she went to the woods and she found out something about herself she had never known. She could move things and without physically touching them.

She was reading into metahumans. And she had books on mutants, and gifted people. All kinds of new age stuff and stories passed on relating to people with certain abilities. She read of an interview someone had done with a man that could light things on fire with no source of ignition in his hand. They had videos of it. Shortly after the videos were brought to the publics' attention the man disappeared never to be heard of again. It was fascinating and even though Evelyn highly disregarded herself as an X-men or an Inhuman, she did know that there was something about her that she couldn't just let go. She was practicing in her house; she was moving cups and plates and sliding tables across the floor. She threw Candy across the room once and after much begging and pleading the collie forgave her. What began as the most traumatic surreal experience of her life soon began to look as one that held great significance in her natural path. She just had to get a better hang of it. She may have had no control with regards to police and harassing phone calls but in the walls of her house she felt she was beginning to gain some form of control and it all started with her mind.

She had begun meditating and eating healthier. She drank only water and tea. No more Coca-Cola or diet Pepsi. The books said she had to be more pure, in a higher state of consciousness to unlock her potential, to really grasp her power. She had to be focused. She had to be in a constant state of now. She had looked into yin and yang. The balance of life and acceptance, things that normally didn't fall into her lap nor even crossed her mind before. It all made sense now.

There was perhaps a new human being coming to light and Evelyn knew without a doubt that she was one of them. She came to believe that his was the type of human that comic books were based off, that were portrayed in movies with red capes and supercars. They say all forms of books and myths, legends and stories all are based off some form of truth. Evelyn believed she had stumbled onto some form of truth yet to be taken seriously. When it did come to light, she wanted to be ready.

So she trained herself. She held strict discipline and as she did her power grew. What she could do was starting to feel more like a blessing than some sort of curse, as she had believed previously because it had killed Todd Johnson.

If you control it, if you understand it, you could come to do amazing things, you could help people and Todd's' life will not have been stopped short for nothing. This is what she told herself each morning and every night. If she truly could master this, she might be able to save people. This was her thought process. She never thought herself as a potential hero but she read once that if you weren't doing something with your life that made other lives easier than you were wasting your time and that had stuck with her. She believed she could do more, so she stayed in the mindset that she could.

At night when the world slept Evelyn found herself in the woods, moving trees and throwing rocks. She'd never uprooted a tree but she felt she could bend them, shift them. Like as if she was moving the space between her hand and an object of her choosing. Not so much as moving the object itself but the air between her hand and the object. If a cup were a foot away and you held your hand in a high-five type of fashion, there would be a foot gap of air between your hand and the cup. Imagine if you could move that air by pushing it, then the cup would move. That's what she found she could do. Move the air. She wanted to test herself but she didn't know how. She also wanted to know if there were others out there like her. But she didn't even know where to start.

It was on a Sunday morning that Evelyn came up with an idea that sounded extremely unorthodox and outstandingly dangerous but that might pay off.

Evelyn had gone to town the day before to get groceries and she decided to stop and grab a poutine on her way home. Despite what the books had said about strict dieting and extreme discipline, she figured that one poutine could not stop her progress. Besides it had been forever since she had something fatty in her diet.

As she waited for her order, sipping her water she saw a Coffee Time paper. Those single sheets with print on both sides that had horoscopes, trivia, quotes and fascinating short stories from around the world on them.

Upon reading it she stumbled on a story about a woman overseas that would dress up as a superhero and literally fight crime. Like a bloody superhero straight out of detective comics. She wore a mask, so no one knew who she was and the public began to call her The Blue Lady or something along those lines. It wasn't the fact that what she was doing was vigilante work and really dangerous but what stood out to Evelyn was that she didn't want praise for it or recognition. It seemed she just wanted to make the world a better place.

That's where Evelyn's idea stemmed from, the Blue Lady vigilante. She wasn't sure how she would do it but she wanted to do something along those lines. If it went according to plan, she would get put in the paper and maybe that would bring the moths to the flames in a sense. At least that's what she was hoping. She didn't know of any other way to bring out any others like her without sounding crazy. She couldn't exactly post it on social media or go around asking people, after all that would be a little hard to do in a city of over a million inhabitants.

The commotion brought on from the Johnson car accident had begun to finally subside after a while so Evelyn felt her life returning to some form of normality and this made her feel more comfortable in going forth with her plan. The lack of police presence constantly monitoring her made it a lot easier to go to and from the city without a drop of suspicion. Evelyn figured this would be the more opportune time to put forth her vigilantism.

She had found a Party City during a trip in and she managed to scrounge up a sort of costume she could wear. Nothing fancy, nothing bulletproof but Evelyn was hoping she wouldn't much worry about flying bullets or knives approaching her. She would start with something less life risking and more in the realm of a burning building where she could run in and do it that way; no vicious criminals to potentially harm her. It seemed like the safer route and after the past weeks, Evelyn could use safe.

It was a Thursday night when Evelyn made her way into the city under the cover of the new moon. She had purchased a police scanner from a pawn shop and waited for the words, "10-15 in progress". Evelyn had found online that a 10-15 was a fire; so her idea was to wait for it, get the address and then she would spring into action.

3:30am on Friday morning she heard the words.

"10-15 in progress. I repeat we have a 10-15...."

Evelyn's legs turned to jelly.

"Holy shit."

She listened for the address, took a deep breath and exhaled.

She showed up as the first firetruck did; mask and all, raring to go. It was a house on fire out in the suburbs. She saw the flames licking the night sky and she knocked the front door down. It didn't take much. She had run in, knocked down a few doors and rescued a dog stuck in a back room. The family had gotten out in time but they had left their German Shepherd in a corner room. The firemen at the scene didn't seem too fond of procuring the canines' safety, so Evelyn did it. After returning the dog to the little boy on the street, Evelyn ran for an alley and bolted back to her car. Heart beating, adrenaline pumping; she had never felt dam alive!

She had scanned the papers in the morning, going through everything hoping to see some mention of her and her abilities. Then she saw the story, buried on page ten of the paper.

Evelyn wasn't complaining, I mean she did technically break the law, but page ten. Come on!

The dad had been quoted as saying," we mustn't have had our doors built properly because we knew that it was a woman and she barely had to touch them and they flew off. She knocked out front door clean into the house!"

Luckily the little boy knew better than his old man.

"She was like Superman! She saved my Lucky!"

Lucky must have been the Shepherd. Well not much mention of her abilities but at least she got some sort of notice.

At the end of the article there was a mention of something. Someone had gotten a video and it would be on the news.

Evelyn flew to her television and scanned the channels waiting for it and she saw it, her glorious entrance on scene.

Her running up the front steps and nailing the door clear off the hinges. The station had slowed it down and there you could see it. They played it in slow motion, rewound it, and played it over and over. No physical touch and yet the door goes rolling into the house. Evelyn had never felt so grateful for television than she did now.

She did it! And she knew she had to do it again.

So here it was at about 11:30pm on a Sunday night a few weeks later and Evelyn found herself sitting in her car in a parking garage looking and feeling halloweenish; waiting for the scanner to justify how weird she felt. There hadn't much going on tonight if her scanner was at all accurate, which she hoped it was.

Waiting patiently.

12:30am rolled onto the dashboard clock and Evelyn was losing hope when suddenly she heard her call.

"Units we have a 10-15 in progress on the corner of 92$^{nd}$ and 39$^{th}$. Apartment fire. Please respond."

Evelyn felt a glimmer of joy which felt wrong being that a fire was taking place, lives were at stake and while she was sure many officers heart dropped and their adrenaline kicked in, Evelyn felt a state of excitement mixed with fear. It felt wrong to her. Still, she remained undeterred.

A quick look up on the address reassured her that the fire wasn't far from her location, which was good because she could leave her car here and walk, no run, to the place. Perfect.

The cool air she found to be relaxing, seeing as her adrenaline had finally kicked in and made her all shaky and nervous. Hopefully no one paid too much attention to her; she would look completely silly right now; running down the street wearing a mask that didn't fit and a costume that was too tight. Please don't make a fool of yourself Evelyn. She bet her parents were looking down at this moment thinking, "where did we go wrong?"

When she rounded the corner of 92$^{nd}$ she saw it, her godsend.

There was the apartment building, a tall one.

God she hoped she knew what she was doing. No turning back now. Evelyn Towne didn't make plans then back out at the last second. No. Evelyn Towne knew what to do and by golly she did it!

There was no sign of flashing lights or sirens to be heard, my god how bad was it that she had literally gotten here by foot and beat any and all emergency vehicles that were to respond. And to think we put the safety of our citizens in the hands of these guys. Unreal she thought.

Focus Evelyn.

There wasn't much smoke billowing from the building, some was coming out of a third, no maybe fourth story window. That's where she would go.

Evelyn Towne to save the day!

Where were the people that should be running out? The little girl at the front screaming, "Please get my Fluffy! Please save him!"

The street and entrance were bare.

First flight of stairs and no people.

Second flight, no one.

Third flight up and not a soul. Should she stop here? No she would on the fourth.

Fourth flight and still no noise anywhere in the building.

Smoke came from under the door that led to the fourth floor hallway. Well at least she had gotten this much right.

She stopped just before opening the door, catching her breath, readjusting this mask of hers. Okay she was ready.

She threw the door open when a thought hit her. Why wasn't there a fire alarm going off? Something wasn't right.

Smoke came from a door about halfway down the hallway and as she approached it, the feeling hit, the pain in her abdomen.

"Not right now. I'm trying to help here. Come on body, cooperate."

She got to the door and without any thought to if somebody were behind it, she blew it off its' hinges and ran through. There she was, she had made her daring rescue attempt. Here she stood, masked crusader to save the day…and yet the apartment stood empty. A table that was falling apart, a couch in the room next to her that was tattered and ragged and not a single noise reverberated off the walls. What the hell?

Then a voice came from somewhere in the darkness of another room.

"Took you long enough….hero."

# Chapter Six

The sun cast its ever warming light onto the water, through the trees, over the hills and burrows and beneath the waves rippling across the surface of the lake. It was a beautiful day all around and Grant Thomas knew exactly what he wanted to do.

"Benny grab your fishing stuff, we're going to get supper!"

"Okay dad!"

The excitement that Grant heard intertwined in his sons reply let him know that this day was going to be special. They had been talking about, planning it, hell maybe even dreaming about it from the moment they saw the ice beginning to melt atop the lake.

"Be sure to bring a sweater son, just in case."

"Already got two packed!"

"Atta boy," he called back to his pride and joy. That boy made him so proud, like he'd finally done something right by Liz. Dam he missed her, especially on days like this.

There were birds singing, bees buzzing, flies flying in and out of the rolled down windows. Grant was grateful that it was nice out today. There wasn't a whole lot they liked to do when the snow covered the ground and they lived where they lived but oh boy when she melted it opened up a whole playground of adventure just waiting to be discovered. That included fishing, boating, tubing, hiking, camping, camp fires, swimming and best of all, at least for the most part besides the obvious boat or tube or boot, it was all free to enjoy. Grant loved the water, he always had, which is why he brought his son up out here and not in some stuffy town. Town life never felt right for him and he imagined just as much for his little boy, his precious Benjamin.

As they rounded a bend in the road Grant saw it, the perfect spot. There was a bridge that went over a large creek that fed into the lake. You could park onto a pull-off spot and you could walk down beside the bridge and even go underneath, it was their favorite place to cast from. This is why Grant always believed God was a fisherman, he made it believable through places just like this one.

Grant had no idea that today would put him on a path that he never would have chosen by himself, if he was ever presented with such a choice. It was April 4$^{th}$.

~

A man and his young son were hauling out fishing gear at the old bridge when Mick drove by with his load of greenfeed. A great many young people frequented that spot, Mick was told it was a nice spot to just sit. It seemed an ideal location but Mick never had time for just sitting.

Mick ran a farm of about 350 head of Murray Grey cattle to the west of the bridge and that consumed most of his days and nights. He had to hire on some hands to help out around the place because unfortunately as Mick grew older, he grew slower and more susceptible to muscle pain and bad knees. Raising cattle was all he knew and he sure as hell wasn't ready to retire or go looking for some desk job in town. Not that anyone was hiring anyway.

It was a scorcher today and when Mick glanced at his thermometer hiding in the shade on the north side of his tac room he read it as 22° Celsius. Not all that bad but he supposed as he grew older perhaps the sun felt hotter to the skin. Funny he thought. You spend all these years getting old, weathering your skin to the elements and in the latter years it up and betrays you. It becomes soft and brittle. Like a dam cracker in soup.

"Sir we have an issue," said a hurried voice to Mick as he was about to sit down on his favorite chair to enjoy the shade for a bit.

The voice came from Bryan or was it Byron? Mick couldn't recall, it was the new guy he just hired on. The kid was smart, hardworking and eager to learn, but he knew just about as much on farming as Mick knew to building rocket ships.

"What's going on kid?"

"Well sir you remember how you said that the creek had slowed down something significant? And that something was probably going on upstream?"

"Get to it son. What'd you find?"

"Beavers built a dam....dam."

"Get my orange bag out of the shop. We'll show those little guys a thing or two. I got some stuff for such the occasion."

"Yes sir, one orange bag coming right up."

Mick knew that old dynamite would come in handy one day. Today was that day. It was April 4$^{th}$.

Over by the lake Grant and his son had gotten to their fishing. They had tied on the lead, hooked on their bait, today they were using leeches and were casting off the east side of the small bridge. Grant watched his boy set up his rod by himself and he couldn't stop thinking about how proud Elizabeth would be right now. Their little man was growing up.

Elizabeth and Grant had met in school, they attended the same classes, had the same group of friends, but it wasn't until grade twelve when they both suddenly realised just how compatible they were together. They had been together ever since.

Elizabeth was outgoing, always laughing and she was smart, she was all around an amazing human being. She'd trade the sweater on her back if you were cold outside, you know, one of those types of people. She was one of those lights, in a dark world and Grant had loved her dearly. He actually brought her to those very spot shortly after they had begun dating. They watched the stars that night from the hood of his car and that was the night he had first kissed her, although she always insisted she had done all the work and kissed him.

After finishing school Elizabeth had stayed pretty close to home and gotten a job at a nursing home in town while Grant had gone the oilfield route. He had started working with a picker truck company and went from slinging tubing to operating a 30 tonne stiff boom in no time. They got a small apartment together and every Saturday night they'd hop in the car and go count stars. They loved driving, especially the two of them, they frequently came to "the spot" as Elizabeth had called it.

Grant had almost proposed to her here but he changed his mind, he wanted their families present when he did, so he had planned to do it at Christmas. Cliché as it was, he knew she would have loved it. At least that was the plan. Grant found though, that plans don't always go as well…planned.

It was about six months before the Christmas proposal when Elizabeth got up one morning in a hurry and ran to the bathroom.

"You okay dear," Grant asked slowly after waiting a bit then following her in.

"I don't know what came over me. I'm going to go to the drugstore after breakfast. Maybe grab some Zantac or something."

"I could go right now and get some if you want, it's no problem."

"No Grant it's okay, let's get some breakfast. I gotta pick up some groceries anyway, I'll do it."

"Ok babe."

They had waffles that morning, with too much syrup and a couple cups of coffee while listening to the radio. It was a beautiful morning despite the fiasco upon awakening but Grant had no idea what that day was actually bringing into their lives.

After returning from her drugstore and grocery run Elizabeth had gone upstairs and while Grant had assumed she was going to change she had actually gone back into the bathroom.

Grant had put the television on by this time and was watching the news. Not much going on in the world that day, he remembered watching something about the summer Olympics, a music awards show and an accident at a campsite in the mountains had caught his eye when he heard the scream from upstairs. Without hesitation he jumped the couch and ran for the stairs.

When he reached the bathroom he threw the door open and there was Elizabeth, standing over the sink holding something in her hand. She turned to look at him and hugged him like she'd never hugged him before.

"You okay? What's going on Liz? You scared the hell outta me just now."

"Grant honey. We're going to be parents."

He recalled the moment in his mind like it had just happened yesterday. Now watching his son it was hard to believe that was ten years ago when that beautiful day occurred. It replayed constantly in his head.

Another day replayed constantly in his head as well…for other reasons. That day occurred nearly nine months after the most beautiful day happened.

"It's happening. Grant honey, this is happening."

Grant was stuck in a book when Liz came out of the kitchen that Wednesday night and uttered those seven words. She was holding her stomach.

"The…the baby you mean?"

"No the second coming, yes I mean the baby!"

"Okay um…go to the car. I'll get the bag."

On the way to the hospital Grant had never felt so dam scared in all his life. It wasn't because he didn't want a child it was because he was afraid he wouldn't be a good dad. The thought alone terrified him, but he would have Liz and he knew the two of them would figure it out together, they always did.

They got to the hospital around eleven o'clock pm. Elizabeth went into this room and Grant was allowed to throw on a gown and hold her hand. No epidural was needed as Elizabeth had suggested they go natural.

"Breathe, just keep breathing Liz. I love you."

Then something felt off, Liz had closed her eyes but they didn't reopen.

"Liz. Liz baby come on, what's wrong?"

"We need another doctor in here, something is going on with the mom," said an orderly yelling out the door.

"What's going on? What's happening," Grant tried asking the nurses.

"Sir we're going to have to ask you to come with us. Ok? Sir please."

"Liz wake up! Baby wake up!"

"Come with me Mr. Thomas, come now we need you out of here."

So Grant had to sit in a chair, just outside and he had to wait. He asked each nurse that went either in or out of the room what was happening and they all said he had to wait to talk to a doctor.

11:30 came by and no word.

11:45 and still no news on his wife and unborn child, this made Grant anxious.

12:00am rolled onto the clock when finally a man in a long white jacket came out.

"Mr. Thomas?"

"Yes that's me. Is everything okay? How's Liz? How's our baby??"

"Sir, your son is in there. He's going to need you. From now on he's going to absolutely need you because I have to tell you something. You won't want to hear this but I need you to think about your son. Ok?"

"Oh god no, please don't…" Grant lost his words.

"Elizabeth didn't make it, I'm so sorry Mr. Thomas. We tried all we could."

In those moments Grant felt something he'd never quite felt before. He felt defeated, almost robbed and it hurt like hell. Images filled his head as he broke down in the hospital hallway. He imagined him and Liz meeting, their first apartment, finding out they had a baby on the way, it all flooded in and Grant cried. He couldn't do this alone.

"Mr. Thomas? Do you want to go in?"

Grant went into the room and straight away he went to the crying baby a nurse was holding.

"Can I? I'm dad."

"Yes sir. You have a beautiful son. Congratulations."

Grant took the child into his arms and as soon as he saw his son, he lost it. He cried and he cried and he laughed. He was a father. He pulled back the blanket by his newborn's head and he looked at him. Grant remembered at that very moment the hospital was empty. It was just him and his little son. Grant had loved him before he even saw him but now that he was in his arms, he'd never realised just how substantial that love was.

"Benjamin. You're Benjamin," Grant had said to the newborn through tears.

"Hey little guy, it's your daddy. I love you my boy. I've been waiting for you."

"I'm going to love you every day," he added.

From that day on Grant had relied heavily on his older sister to help him with the parenting of his lovely son. Some nights when he stood there, crying baby in his arms, not a clue in the world what to do, he would think of Liz. He could see her in his son, her eyes, her nose and it brought him back to why he was where he was. The beautiful baby in his hands needed him; he needed his dad to be strong and to raise him as best as he could. So Grant thought to himself on the days he felt too lonely, yes he had lost the love of his life, but he always had a part of her, in his son. Liz had given her life to allow Ben to live. Grant was to give him just that, a life and a beautiful one at that.

Mick and Bryan had trekked through some small bush to get to the beaver dam but when Mick saw the animal house responsible for flooding his pasture he knew they had been at this one for a minute or two. The bloody thing was a dam good size, no wonder it had slowed his creeks. Mick was for a moment impressed, but only for a moment, then it was back to the need to blow these sons of guns out of the water.

"Okay, here's the plan," Mick said to Bryan already knowing the plan was simple. Place and then light and finally boom.

"We'll set the sticks at some structural places and by we, I mean you, there's no way in hell I'm going to get on and off that thing. Don't worry you won't fall through, just start on the far side. Light then place and make your way back this way. You'll have plenty of time. I got the long fuses on these puppies."

"Uhh…alright sir. I'll do it. Probably a bad time to ask for a raise I'm guessing?"

"Ha. I like you kid, you got spunk. Alright, if you do this and that big bastard lets loose the tide, I'll think about increasing your pay. How's that sound?"

"Got a light sir?"

"Atta boy. Now don't drop that, it used to be the wife's."

Just downstream from where Old Mick and Bryan were attempting to blow a beaver house sky high, Grant and his boy had been fishing for a couple hours now.

"Dad I'm going to go scout under the bridge for some cool rocks to add to my collection."

"Ok son but make sure to come out once in a while and say hi to me alright?"

"Yes dad. I will," replied his son as he disappeared under the bridge.

Grant reached for more bait. Dam it was empty. Good thing he picked up some more. You really could not be too careful when it came to matters such as this.

"I need to re-bait this in the…" Grant didn't finish his sentence when he heard a bang in the distance.

What the hell was that he thought to himself? Bet it was those dam seismic guys.

"Alright where are you Mr. Orange container," Grant said aloud to himself as he rummaged through the stuff in the trunk of his car. He'd wanted to clean it out for some time now but he always decided not to. He basically knew where everything was in there, it just took some searching. He hadn't realised Ben put the new container of bait in the front seat after pulling up here.

"I just put you in here I swear, where the hell are you," Grant argued into the trunk. Then he saw it.

Liz's blue necklace, the one she would wear when they went out. God she looked beautiful in it, though she looked beautiful in everything if truth were to be told. Grant thought back to the last time they had gone for supper before Liz had gotten too pregnant to go out as she used to say. He was thinking of how he looked at her that night and how she looked back. They talked about the first kiss, as they usually did, they talked about the nursery, and names. Whether they thought they would have a beautiful girl or a handsome son. Then something made him double over.

He got a turning feeling in his stomach and he felt he couldn't catch his breath. That's when he came back to earth and he heard it. The sudden pick up in the water movement; he could hear it hitting the bridge. It felt cold all of a sudden.

Ben.

Grant struggled to get to his feet, he still couldn't quite breathe right and suddenly he felt his body go weightless. The strength came back into his legs and he ran down the hill and under the bridge.

"BENNY!"

He scanned under the bridge but there was no sign of his little boy.

Where'd he go? Where the hell did he go?

And as Grant looked around he got a glimpse of a shadowed object against the middle pillar about halfway under. Without a second thought Grant jumped for it.

The speed of the water surprised him when he went under, it fought to push him east. He fought back and through the muddied water he reached out. Clutching to the dirt, pulling back weeds. He kept fighting.

And suddenly his hand touched something. Cold. Unmoving. Pinned against the pillar.

Benjamin.

He braced his feet on the slippery side of the pillar, clutched his boy in both arms and pushed as hard as he could towards the sky.

He broke the surface just off the side of the bridge.

"No, no not again. Not my Benny."

He trudged through and got to the shore.

His son had gone pale; no breath came from his lungs.

"If you take my little boy I swear to god."

He pushed down on his son's chest, he breathed into his mouth.

"Come on Benny. Come on wake up. Daddy needs you."

He raced to the car and dialed 911.

He returned to his son and kept compressions. He kept breathing for him.

"Come on son, please don't leave me."

"Daddy needs you. Please come back."

Grant tried so hard. He never gave up on his boy.

He went until his arms burned.

When he finally stopped he felt what he told himself he would never feel again.

Helpless.

"NOOOOOOOO!!"

As Grant collapsed and closed his eyes, he heard a large crunching noise in the background.

Then his world turned black.

He saw Elizabeth. She was hugging Benny. The three of them then hugged all together.

"We're okay Grant. You have to go back now and find them. It's important. Wake up."

Grant opened his eyes.

"He's regained consciousness. The father, look his eyes are open."

"Sir, we need you to stay calm. We got you, you're okay."

Grant turned his head to the side…he was in an ambulance.

To his immediate left there was another gurney. A sheet covered whoever lay under it.

Benjamin.

Grant closed his eyes again as he fell back into the dark.

# Chapter Seven

7:09am.
    Eiri had beaten his alarm clock to the punch by about an hour and twenty minutes this morning, which he guessed was better than the typical four hours or so that he usually had it down to. Way to go Eiri. Way to stay positive.

Eiri looked at the calendar hanging by his bedside table, it was Saturday. What in the hell was he going to do at 7 in the morning on a Saturday? Blast this dam internal clock of his, he should get a new one.

Coffee, he was always ready for coffee though.

And….eggs, hmm that was odd. Eiri hadn't wanted eggs since… well since her. Eggs was her thing, she absolutely loved them. Every morning it was scrambled eggs with that woman.

Alright yeah, Eiri could go for some eggs.

The sizzling of eggs on frying pan kept him from falling asleep as the aroma of dark roast slowly readied in the background. Eiri put on some music every time he was doing something in the kitchen because he had read once, "cook with love".

For some reason, despite the tons of useless information his brain liked to store in case Eiri would wind up a contestant on a game show, it kept "cook with love" front and center. Thanks brain. It waited there with an article he read once on "how to correctly do the Heim…. Heimlich?" Sounds German, maybe he spelled it right. Eiri had to have a dictionary somewhere. If he didn't find the correct spelling it'd drive him batty all dam day.

Heimlich maneuver spelled correctly and old Henry was definitely not German.

As he sat and ate his scrambled eggs and cheese while drinking his coffee Eiri thought back to the last time he had eaten a thing of scrambled eggs.

Eiri had woken up that morning in a bit of a haze. His head rang slightly and his eyes took longer than usual to adjust to the morning light sneaking in around his curtained window. But wait. It smelled terrific once his nose decided to wake up. She was making breakfast.

He had walked out of his bedroom and proceeded around the corner to the kitchen area. There she stood, like an angel, his angel.

"Good morning sleepy,"

"Good morning to you pretty lady."

"How are you feeling? You look like hell," she laughingly pointed out while he made a cup of java.

"That's about how I felt, until I saw you."

"Well played. Good answer hon," she said as she began dishing their plates.

"You're amazing. You know that?"

"Thanks hon. Here, eat something. You'll feel better.

Eiri remembered that the eggs that morning tasted like gold; he remembered she looked beautiful in that morning light. He also remembered thinking that he could do that every morning, forever, for as long as he lived.

After breakfast they went for a walk through the park. They stopped by the pond at one point and she had promised him she would never leave him. She said that they'd grow old and do this walk all the time. She said that he was stuck with her.

She lied.

Eiri snapped back to reality as his cup of dark roast ended.

8:30 now.

This was about the time he took his morning walk. It helped calm the anger inside and it was after all, not court mandated.

Court mandated therapy. Crock of shit that was to begin with.

It was awhile back at a store, a store he had gone to a thousand times before the incident. It was just a regular day going onto a regular afternoon in the middle of a regular damn week. Eiri went in to find something to sip on, to quench the thirst if you will, when he saw him. Him being the guy she had met up with before…well before she left.

He was just going on with his life, buying a sandwich, looking through a newspaper with no idea what had happened. He didn't know what went through his head at that moment but Eiri know he reached a point of rage where he thought that guy knew something. That he was responsible. So he went up to him.

This is where the surveillance footage took over because you couldn`t hear the words that were exchanged between the two men that day and for the life of him Eiri couldn't recall what he'd said anyway and although he hadn't seen the footage, apparently it would show that Eiri didn't touch the guy. Case in point.

Something Eiri couldn't know at the time was that the surveillance footage did indeed show the altercation and as much as he denied it, Eiri deserved what he'd gotten.

In fact the guys over at the department couldn't stop playing it over and over.

"Ok here have the perp. Oh see that? He recognizes the victim. He's contemplating and contemplating and he turns around but then against better judgement he decides to talk to the vic."

"This is where it gets interesting."

The video showed Mal's Convenience at about 10:00 in the morning on a Wednesday. It showed Eiri walk in after Greg had showed up, Greg being the guy who is the "victim" in this case.

It shows Eiri casually walk up to the beverage cooler and then he notices Greg and decides to engage a conversation which if Eiri recalled a little began with, "hey asshole."

The video has no audio but from subtle body language you can decipher that it gets real awkward real fast. And it also shows Greg shove him. First contact came from him, which in turn would make Eiri's actions self defense right?

True…if you don't completely lose it on the guy.

After Greg shoves him, something odd happens.

"Watch the lights now Sir," a constable says to his captain over at Precinct 425.

The whole video dims as the lights go out for an instance and a large surge of something fires into Greg's torso.

It knocks him flying back through shelves and into an ATM.

It leaves Eiri curled in a ball with his hands over his head, like the roof was going to collapse.

From this footage, some judge determined Eiri shoved Greg super hard and he just went flying, because to hell with the actual physics of this particular altercation right? This all granted him an assault charge and it granted Greg a few broken ribs and a concussion.

And being at the time Eiri did not remember any of this, he agreed seeing as how this did seem like something he would do and hell if there was a video of it, than well.

So where would he walk to this morning?

It was almost 9 by the time he felt human enough to even consider going walking, and although he did feel a bit anxious this morning he figured screw it, after all it was nice out.

The cool air felt invigorating as Eiri walked out of his apartment building; it was a beautiful day outside. What a perfect morning, and as an added bonus there was no dam people to deal with.

Little did Eiri know that within fifteen minutes of that moment, his life would change forever.

Eiri reached Whyte Ave and began to walk west to avoid getting the sun in his eyes because although it wasn't boiling hot outside, it was still pretty dam bright for one's retinas.

The street was pretty dead that morning and even the buses seemed less full than usual. Every few minutes a car would go by and Eiri only saw a handful of people out and about shopping. Which is why when the black cars showed up, he thought nothing of it.

Eiri didn't know for how long or if they'd been following him but when he reached the empty lot just off Gateway, they pulled in and cut him off.

"That's the dam guy."

Eiri knew that voice. Greg.

Four or five men got out of the vehicles and surrounded Eiri.

Then the punching started, and then the kicking.

Eiri didn't stand a chance and within seconds he was on the ground being pummeled.

"Not so tough now huh?"

"They never are when their time comes."

Amidst the pain and the shuffling noises Eiri began thinking to himself, "this isn't how my life was supposed to go. I was supposed to be someone; I was supposed to be important. We were supposed to get married. She wasn't supposed to go!"

And then something.....well something incredible happened.

The loose dirt on top of the ground rose about a foot into the air, it held suspended for a second or two and then it slammed back down and as it did Eiri rose up and the men surrounding him went flying. The two cars went up on two wheels and landed back onto all four. Everything around him moved back about thirty feet.

As he stood there, fists clenched, breathing heavily while covered in blood, Eiri saw him. He was in the backseat of a Cadillac, looking out the window at him, eyes wide in fear.

Greg.

Eiri reached towards the car and without actually touching it he ripped the door off and threw it to the side. Then still being twenty feet away Eiri pulled Greg out of the car so he was suspended in front of him by some unseen force then Eiri lifted Greg up into the air and slammed him into the ground so hard that he left a crater. Then he looked around at the scene surrounding him. And he ran.

What the hell had he just done?

Eiri felt like he'd just finished a dam triathlon but he kept running. Eiri ran all the way home and he wasn't sure what he was going to do when he got there but he couldn't be outside anymore. He had to go away for a little bit.

When he reached his apartment he hurriedly packed some clothes, a tent and a sleeping bag.

Eiri was getting the hell out of town.

He had to figure out what he had just done and if was getting stronger. He had to control it and he knew just the place to do it.

The self-storage unit Eiri had rented wasn't ever really touched and although it was full of things, he never made the trip out to it to check on them. Today Eiri did though.

His father's old bike sat in it. That was Eiri's ticket out of here and luckily an old friend taught him how to ride awhile back.

What the hell was happening to him?

# Chapter Eight

Benjamin Ryder was never really fond of road trips, not at all. He couldn't figure out why it was fun being stuck in a small cab for hours on end. How was that fun? It was Alberta and after growing up here, truth be told there wasn't a very high rate of diversification when it came to the scenic nature. Sure, it was beautiful but it was either the land had trees or it didn't. The Rockies to the West were the true reason people came to this province. But this was Northern Alberta. Ben and Jeremy had been driving down the 63 after pulling through Fort Mac for a while now and guess what Ben had seen? Trees, lots of them, and traffic, lots of it.

They were headed to the big mill in Northern Alberta. They had passed a smaller family run business north of The Mac but the boss insisted they go to the bigger one to unload and then they'd drive to the city from there. It was drive out day. Soon they'd be at home, home sweet home.

"That cheap bastard has to maintain this dam truck of his. The brakes are catching again. Man why doesn't his overpaid ass do these last drives," Jeremy asked Ben in an angered tone.

"He's the experienced one behind the wheel of this thing," he added.

"Because then he'd have all the fun man," Ben answered, grinning as he did.

Sometimes Ben enjoyed stirring the pot.

"You should be a comic Mr. Ryder. You're super funny."

"Nah, I get nervous in front of people."

"Excuses. You just don't like people."

"Haha yah well you can't blame me Jeremy. People are weird."

"I'll give you that one man, people sure can be weird. Actually that reminds me of something I wasn't sure how to bring up before but this seems appropriate."

"Oh boy this will be good. It's about her isn't it?"

Jeremy turned a bit red at the mention of "her".

"Yes. Sort of. Just hear me out."

"I'm listening Jerr. I am. Go ahead."

"Okay well it's been a long fucking year. A tough one with you know the divorce and all. But I just wanted to say that through it all, you kept me pretty level-headed. Stop looking at me like that, I'm not going to buy you roses or some shit Ben so f off."

"Haha I'm bugging you man, I know what you're trying to say. We've been friends forever man, that's what friends do."

"So thanks for that Benny. It really helps. That crazy bitch almost had me," Jeremy said through a half laugh.

"Look at you, almost laughing about it. That's the Jeremy I know, tough as nails."

"You're alright Ben Ryder. You're alright."

"That's what your ex-wife said," Ben cracked back as he burst out laughing.

"I take that all back now," Jeremy replied.

The two bantered back and forth as they drove on. The twin lanes seemed overly busy today and Ben kept wondering if it was a long weekend or not. He never kept up with all these new holidays that popped up all the time, it seemed pointless. He remembered Christmas, New Years, Canada Day and Easter. Those were the good ones in Ben's mind.

"Hey buddy did you catch that article in the paper we grabbed from that Husky?"

Ben looked back to Jeremy questioningly.

"Okay guess not, well read it, it's interesting as hell," Jeremy said as he reached back for it, "it's on page 8."

Ben began flipping through the pages until he hit page 8. The title read, "The Masked Lady".

"The Masked Lady?"

"Read it man."

"Like out loud or?"

"God Ben I mentioned it to you, don't you think I've already… oh you're real funny."

Ben scanned the article about a lady in the city who dressed up in some blue costume and helped out at a house fire.

"So she's a vigilante?"

"No Benny, she's a superhero."

"Let's see. Takes it upon herself to deal with something that perhaps the proper authorities should have dealt with, that's a vigilante. Oh wait she saved a dog. She's a firefighter man. In a costume."

"Ben come on, let her have her day. She's a hero."

"My grandpa served. That's a hero."

"I hear you Ben, I do. But I still think she's doing something pretty outstanding. There's a ton of bad things and bad people that happen to this world. I think someone stepping up and doing something about it is really something. I hope she's still out there."

"Hey Jeremy there's a video. Where's your phone at, I'll YouTube it."

It didn't take long before he saw it. It had a lot of views and it'd only been up a short time.

"Describe it to me, I'm not pulling over."

Ben clicked play.

"Ok the video started and the house is in full view, flames and smoke barreling up into the night sky. A family is standing just off the sidewalk and the youngest of them is pointing towards the house and jumping. Kid seems pretty upset. Whoa out of nowhere a lady is running by them full tilt towards the house. Yup that's a full on fucking costume, I think her mask is about to fall off."

"Ok what else?"

"Ok she's running up to the front door and…holy shit."

"What, what happened, did she fly?"

"No one is flying but... hang on I'm going to rewind it quickly and see that again."

Ben watched it again and again. She didn't touch the door but yet it is knocked off its hinges and flies into the darkness of the house.

"Jerr she just moved the door, without touching it."

"What? But how?"

"I don't know man. Oh and now she's out, she grabbed a dog and now she's off running away again. What the hell did I just watch?"

Jeremy looked at Ben and a smile slowly spread across his face.

"Superhero."

The era of the superhero Ben thought. Interesting.

Ben didn't know why but seeing the video triggered something in his memory and he faded back to a time when he was younger. The incident.

Ben must have been about sixteen or so at the time and he never could explain what exactly had transpired but it felt connected to what he just watched. He felt it.

He and Jeremy had been out one night doing what sixteen year olds do and this was shortly after Jeremy had gotten his license. It was a Friday night and they'd had one too many Cold Shots when Jeremy decided they'd better head home before his father called and bitched about the car being out too late. After another beer Ben agreed. Home wasn't far away and it was out of town, all they had to do was get out of town without the cops seeing them and they were home free. Nothing but backroads after they left the town limits.

There was the bridge ahead now so that meant they were in the clear because once they crossed the bridge it was just a small ways until the turn off onto the township road. This deserved a beer Ben thought and they may as well have another, they were almost home.

"Don't kill me, I'm going to climb back and grab a beer. You want?"

Jeremy didn't answer.

"Suit yourself man," Ben said as he climbed over the front seat and reached for the case sitting in the backseat.

"I can't reach them, can we pull over quickly?"

Jeremy didn't answer again.

"Jerr man what the hell," Ben said loudly as he squirmed around so he was facing forward again.

Jeremy had fallen asleep. They were headed for the river.

"Jeremy wake up!"

But Jeremy didn't stir. They had gone into the ditch now and managed to miss the guardrail, Ben knew that they'd plough through the trees and with the momentum of the car they would reach the river.

The car shook and jumped as it ran over dirt and grass and Ben scrambled to get into the front seat again. Something caught his foot.

"What the hell, come on, come on. I don't want to die."

His foot wouldn't move.

"Shit, shit, shit," was all Ben could say.

The darkness of the river was growing.

"NOOOOOOOO," Ben yelled out and as he did grass flew onto the windshield and dirt shot upwards like a geyser of water.

The car slammed to a stop.

Ben remembered thinking at that moment that he was dead. His body had released some chemical to ease the dying process and this was it.

After a minute of his hands checking his body for bumps or blood or anything, Ben realised he wasn't dead. They'd actually stopped.

"Jerr?"

A groaning noise meant he was alive.

"Oh thank god."

Dust like particles filled the cab, an airbag had gone off. Jeremy's to be exact.

"What the hell," he mumbled slowly.

"You okay man?" Ben asked.

"What'd you do to my dad's car man?"

"What'd I…no no no. This was you buddy. But it's okay, you're alive, I'm alive. Look ahead."

Jeremy unclicked his belt and climbed out, Ben followed from the back. They stood within half a football field of the river. They'd been stopped by a spot of raised earth.

"My dad is going to kill us man."

"Probably man but at least we're alive."

Ben looked down at his hands, they were hot and they hurt.

"I'm going to call my dad Ben. He'll come for us."

"Okay brother, okay."

Ben was in a thought back in the past but he came back to the current time as Jeremy loudly pointed out that this was their turn.

"Alrighty we are almost done here man, we're almost home Ben!"

"Okay brother, okay," Ben replied.

The last of their road trip to Lac La Biche was rather quiet, both men seemingly lost in thought.

Interesting was all Ben could think to himself. Rather interesting indeed.

Superhero.

# Chapter Nine

William S. Watson was a full time firefighter. He lived a modest life, in a modest house, on a modest street in a very modest neighborhood in south Edmonton. Each day he woke up and ate warm oatmeal with exactly two cups of coffee, anymore cups made him jittery. He had a quick shower, didn't always wash his hair, brushed his teeth and walked out his door by 7:22AM. He then arrived at the station for about 7 minutes to 8:00AM. He was never too early, nor too late. William S. Watson was a man of discipline; William S. Watson was a man to depend on.

He'd always gotten good grades throughout elementary school and maintained them straight through to graduation, Will was a quick study when it came to learning new skills. It didn't seem to matter what he was doing, if it interested him, he excelled at it. Be that as it may, it came as a bit of a surprise to the rest of the family when Will had wanted to follow his dad's footsteps with firefighting rather than go off to a good university somewhere. Will knew this was his life and he knew he only got one. So he followed what he wanted to do, rather than what was expected of him. And when his old man passed away of cancer, he told William just how proud of him he was. That made it all worth it to Will.

"Good morning Will, how goes the battle this morning," Will was asked as he came into the station and walked up to Ed Keller.

"Morning Ed, it goes great and you?"

"Beautiful morning can't complain. Did you see the news?"

"I haven't. Oh no what happened now?"

"No, no. It was nothing bad. Well kinda. Read the paper in the breakroom. It's on page four."

MASKED LADY SAVES FAMILY DOG

What is this about William wondered as he picked up the paper sitting on the cluttered break room table. Why were there always ten copies of things no one ever read on this table?

Will scanned through the story Ed had mentioned. A lady goes into a burning house and saves a dog but the biggest thing on people's mind was how she "telekinetically" moved the entryway door clear off its hinges without laying a single finger on it.

"Did you read it?"

"Yes Ed. Pretty crazy thing happened there eh?"

"I'd say so. Made us all look like damned fools."

"I'm sorry what," William asked back, unsure why he looked a fool right now.

"We should have gotten the dam dog."

"Well, I mean, we got the people out."

"Yeah, but you know how it is, dam camera phones always watching. There's hero lady saving the day and boom there's four of our best, scratching our asses. Media is kicking our butt right now."

"That darn social media thing can be a bit of a beast with public image ya know?"

"Here, here Ed. I hear ya. Well about that time eh," William mentioned. He was trying to get away from talking with Ed. He liked Ed but he just didn't want to talk this morning. He felt something. Something off.

"So it is Will. I'll catch you later."

"Later Ed."

William S. Watson then proceeded with his usual day. Clean up the spot a bit, organize his suit in the perfect way to maximize efficiency should ever an emergency arise and haste be needed, he also tidied up the truck as best he could.

He hadn't been at the station for too long when a call came in and the alarms went off. A warehouse was being consumed in the east and time was of the essence.

William S. Watson was ready. What William didn't know was that this fire would forever change his life as he knew it and for that, William S. Watson wasn't ready.

The crew flew together to leave the station was quick as they could, and within minutes they were tearing down the road already on their way to the warehouse in need. Traffic wasn't too bad today and that gave William the chills. Why this gave him the chills he wasn't overly sure but it did nonetheless.

"There's the beast, you know what that means. Go time gentlemen."

William took the Chief's words in as he controlled his breathing, one of his pre-job rituals.

The truck rolled onto the street and instantly the smoke was noticeable, the smell, the burn.

"Westin and Wesley you go in now, check for stragglers. Hanley and Turk you come with me. Let's bring this big bastard down a size or two."

"Yes sir," was the collective reply.

"Westin keep up," Wesley said as he and Will came up to the third floor checks.

They'd been doing a quick routine sweep of each level of the building, it'd been empty thus far and as they ascended, the smoke grew thicker.

On the fifth floor up, William got a strange sensation in his head. A queasiness spread over him and he felt very faint all of a sudden, he stumbled to grab something as he tried to keep up to Wesley.

"Hey Wes hold up, not feeling a hundred percent here."

Wesley slowed and came back around to Will.

"Hey man, what's the deal, you good?"

"Wes there's something going on with my head man, making my hands all numb and crap."

"What the hell does that mean?"

"I gotta go back down man."

"Okay well let me radio the Chief really quick and….."

The wall of flame barreled over on the two men before either of the two knew it was coming and the floor beneath them gave way. The two men fell down into the raging inferno, down into the make shift Hell that had, unbeknownst to them, been forming in the center of the burning out building; beneath them.

~

Ed Keller had been fire chief for eight years. He'd followed in his father's footsteps in that aspect, and he was damn proud he had done it. He had promised his dear father on his deathbed that he'd make Chief and after years of hard work and two failed marriages, Ed did it. Now he wasn't sure what to do with himself most days. Until today, Ed knew what to do today.

The crew pulled up to the giant warehouse and Ed gave out a quick set of orders. As he, Hanley and Turk prepared the truck for a counterattack he wondered if sending in Westin and Wesley was a good idea, he should have gone with either of them. After all this was a bad one, he felt it.

The men hadn't been on site for too long when the building fought back with one last hay maker. A loud whooshing sound followed by what felt like a wave of heat straight out of Hell itself shot out from the second floor. Ed Keller instantly thought, this was it, it was a backdraft. The heat burnt out the middle of the structure and the beast began to come down on itself.

Ed's thoughts then traveled to that of his men, Westin and Wesley.

There wasn't any time for anyone to do anything when they realised what had happened.

Ed Keller didn't feel too good.

The crew waited hours for all the hot spots to dissipate. Large machinery was brought in to knock over the parts of the structure that presented a hazard to personnel.

Ed went through the building once presented the chance to do so; he had to look for them. He had to.

Nothing but ash and failed framing falling into piles of rubble, the place was devastated. Room by room Ed and his crew scoured the debris, looking for any kind of remnant of his valiant men.

Damn this city and its warehouse fires Ed thought in his head. His dad had battled the original warehouse disaster years and years ago. He too, lost men that day. Ed couldn't believe he was getting the same luck his father had before him. It was almost surreal.

Ed came around into the scattered remains of what looked to be a bathroom slash shower room kind of thing towards the back of the main floor. An old cracked bathtub sat in a corner.

Nothing survived a fire he thought, not even a damn porcelain bathtub remained complete.

"Well boys, let's go home. We got phone calls to figure out."

The crew couldn't believe they'd lost two men as fast as they just did, it all didn't seem quite real.

"DAMMIT," Turk yelled out.

"Turk," said a weakened voice from the cracked bathtub so low it was barely audible.

Ed turned and ran for the tub; he threw the half that had fallen in on itself.

There curled in a ball, buck naked, was William Watson.

# Chapter Ten

Grant wasn't good at loss, or grief or any of the "negative" emotions we humans frequented so damn much. Although perhaps no one was truly good at any of them either, there were people however, who knew just what to say and do in those types of situations, and Grant wasn't one of them. Grant grew angry, like he'd been cheated in this life. First Elizabeth was taken, and now Ben. None of it made sense, what had Grant done so damn bad in his life that he deserved any of the feelings he was currently feeling? The anger slowly filled his bones as it fused with confusion and that left the man even more of a mess. And the man retreated into himself.

The bridge accident, that after much deliberation was found to be caused by some farmer blowing up a dam, ended up fetching Grant a pretty sizeable settlement, you know with the bridge breaking and all. That was the official statement as to what happened, the water caused the bridge to break on Benjamin and the blame fell to the county and not so much to the old farmer. So in all his misdirected misfortune, Grant quit his job and hid away at his house. He'd had enough of the world.

The door opened slowly, creaking as it slid slowly above the barren wooden floor. The sound echoed off the empty walls, throughout the hollowed out rooms. The house was a four bedroom and it was a hell of a good price when Grant and Elizabeth saw the advertisement for it. Now only one bedroom was being used most days, Grant's room. It was his prison and his sanctuary. This was his space to comfortably fall apart.

A small black RCA flat screen sat on a dresser at the foot of the queen sized bed set up just right so that Grant could sit up and reach the command buttons on the right side. To his left he had set up a small television table where his cups could go and it also provided space for his plates of sandwiches he decided to live off of. Sandwiches, granola bars, caffeine and noodles. This was how he'd go out Grant figured. Maybe some sort of poetic justice would come by and make his heart stop. Maybe he'd be in some internet link on a page somewhere in the future, claiming he'd died of a broken heart, maybe they wouldn't be wrong.

A voice came over the speakers as Grant ate his ham and cheese. The voice was that of a news anchor and he was joined by a woman, they spoke on the weather, sports and of course the worldly happenings that occurred today. A whole lot of nothing happened today, that's what happened.

A plastic cracking noise sounded out loudly in the house as Grant opened his bottle of whiskey, it was louder than the current television volume.

The cold drink brought Grant to the ground, he felt himself feeling more floaty-feeling than not these days, like he wasn't physically attached to the earth anymore and if he willed it, some days he thought he could just float away. Up, up away. Disconnected like a bad plug.

By eleven that evening the whiskey had taken its hold of Grant's psyche and he faded out like a forgotten candle. And as he fell, he dreamed things. Things he couldn't explain, like dark things, ugly things, and things not of this world.

He woke in his room, covered in a sweat. The clock had gone out, or at least it must have because the illuminated red numbers weren't at all visible in the darkened room. Given the blanket of the shadow that hid his house from his eyes, Grant felt safe to assume it was still late in the night.

A chill filled the air. Why was it so still?

Grant was suddenly overwhelmingly famished so he stumbled around until he found a small flashlight that sat on his dresser for instances such as this. Don't expect the worst but prepare for it, score one Grant.

As he made his way down the darkened stairs he couldn't help but wonder why in the hell the air felt so different. It was making the hair on his arms stand up and suddenly his mouth felt dry. When he reached the bottom of the staircase he could see streetlight pouring in through his front door. Meaning it was open, why the hell was it open? Had he forgotten it the night prior? He had been drinking fairly heavy, maybe he wanted fresh air or some crap at an awkward hour? Grant pondered to himself, maybe he'd suddenly remembered to check….a blood curling scream quickly shattered the silence of the night.

Grant dropped his cup. He lunged forward for the door to peer his head outside. The moonlight brightly illuminated his yard and fortunately it lay empty.

The cool air caught him off guard when he stepped out into the world outside his small hideaway. Which is precisely why hearing a scream wasn't exactly normal. He lived in the bush, he really shouldn't be hearing anyone or anything this far out.

The scream rang out again. And a faint noise could be heard behind everything. A whistle?

"North and like West…ish," Grant said out loud to himself. Trying to pinpoint which direction it was coming from. Grant realised how alone he was. Why the hell hadn't he ever gotten a dog?

His palms were growing clammy, so he wiped away the cold sweat onto his pant leg.

HONK. HONK. BEEP. BEEP.

Grant had managed to bump his car keys in his pocket and set off his car's alarm and horn.

"Shit. Shit."

He shut off his car, of course he was standing right in front of the bloody thing when it went off and now he was certain he had a code brown.

"Goddamn automobile and your stupid horn and your dumb sticker," Grant said as he slapped his car's bumper as if to make it feel his anguish towards it.

"Honk If You're On the Path."

"Yeah I'm on the path to going in my pants."

Weapon, yes now that's a good idea man. What do we got? Shed. Yes it'll have something. Grant spoke out loud when he was nervous, it helped him follow his thoughts a little more cohesively.

The whistling noise could be heard off in the distance, it grew slowly louder. Grant couldn't understand was happening around him, he was afraid but that scream came from someone who may need help.

Given his current mental status being what it was, that some would describe as a bit rocky, his reactions and ability to want to help surprised himself. Rake? No. No not a hoe either or a post hole auger. A crow bar might do it but then Grant saw a wrecking bar tucked away in a back corner. That would do even better, light but solid.

Grant was rummaging through the cluttered mess of his shed, reaching for his weapon of choice when his house exploded beside him. Grant was thrown through his shed and knocked unconscious almost instantaneously.

Something in the air, it hung and covered everything. What was that god awful ringing noise? Grant's head felt like it was about to erupt and his eyes hurt as warm liquid ran slowly down his face and Grant knew he had to get back to his feet. What the hell had just happened?

He felt the flashlight bounce off his right foot, the sliding noise it made allowed Grant to feel for it and pick it up.

The beam of light was stopped short by a wall of dust and broken building. Luckily the moon was still bright, meaning Grant hadn't been out too terribly long.

A loud boom from above made Grant drop to the ground and cover his head, suddenly his paradise had turned into what sounded like a bloody warzone.

No explosion followed the loud noise so Grant looked around. Nothing stirred but the dust particles caught on the night breeze. He had to get up and get gone. Where? He didn't know, he wasn't even sure as to what was going on. Maybe it was the Russians.

He struggled to find his feet as he leaned on a wall of his shed, the ground beneath him looked oddly magical as the moonlight lit up the fallen dust. Then the ground went dark. Grant looked slowly upwards.

The ship was massive. Dark and square in shape, it had something suspended below it, another ship maybe?

Grant couldn't get his brain to follow what his eyes were seeing, the object floated right over him and continued towards the west. It was carrying a large dome. The sides of the dome had stuff falling down it. Grant couldn't make out what it was that was dropping off though. What was happening right now?

A loud rustling noise came from the trees to the north of where Grant stood huddled by what used to be his house.

Thud. Thud. Thud.

It sounded like large footsteps now.

Thud. Thud. Thud.

It got closer to Grant.

Thud. Thud. Thud.

Grant braced himself.

From out of the treeline a large spiderlike creature came bounding out towards Grant, it's mouth open, pincer like things on either side gnashing repeatedly and making the most horrendous of noises, it knew Grant was there; it lunged straight for him.

Grant hit the floor with a loud bang. He'd rolled off his bed and into his table.

He opened his eyes and saw his roof over him, his walls stood intact on each side.

"That was a dream…holy hell."

Grant got to his feet and lay back on his bed, after a drink he was able to fall back to sleep and when he did he dreamed of things, bad things.

# Chapter Eleven

Ed Keller's retirement party was held just two months after the devastating warehouse fire that claimed the life of his co-worker and friend, Peter Wesley. His funeral then followed shortly after.

The days that followed the incident, as the men in suits so poetically called it, were full of small rooms with no windows and questions beyond questions. And none that made sense to Ed. Where did Will come from? Did we notice a change in his personality? Was he hanging out with anyone new? Ed didn't honestly know half of the answers to any of them anyways, for the most part William kept to himself and Ed respected his bubble. A lady who evidently wanted to die from lung cancer was present the whole time Ed was questioned. She sat quietly in the corner. And she just smoked cigarette after cigarette, with barely a break. If Ed was any kind of smoker perhaps he'd have been impressed.

The smoking lady stood up at one point after what seemed like days and walked over to the table where Ed had been trapped. She made eye contact with Ed and took a long drag off her Du Maurier cigarette. Fancy broad.

"So you understand the importance of what we're asking you to do right Mr. Keller?"

"I do."

"And what do we want you to do Mr. Keller?"

"You want me to lie. You want me and what's left of my crew to say that they both died."

"Precisely. Easy peasy, no? Okay so you and the boys do just that, and you'll never see us again. But if you or any.."

"Where is he," Ed asked, cutting her short of what she was saying. The lady smiled at him.

"We have him in containment, that's all I am at liberty to say right now."

The smoking lady stared intently at Ed, as if she was making an attempt at reading his mind. Although after what he had just witnessed, he wouldn't be as taken aback….probably.

"Just let us go home."

"Yes sir. Quick sign right there," the lady gestured to Ed she was holding a clipboard extended towards him, on it was clipped a document. Ed grabbed the pen and signed the paper.

"Perfect now we're right as rain Mr. Keller."

"Who are you people," Ed asked before he was escorted out of the room.

"Don't you worry about that Mr. Keller. We're the good guys."

Ed and his men, Turk and Hanley, walked out into the moonlight when they were finally allowed to leave. They'd been in there too long and no words were said between the men when they went their separate ways; they knew what they'd just agreed to and without saying they all knew not one of them was fully right with it.

Ed got home that night and when he glanced at his microwave the small digital numbers announced that it was one thirty three in the morning. He went straight up to his bedroom and fell right to sleep.

He never returned to the station, neither of the three ever did. Ed did attend the planned retirement party that the crew threw together for him though, he owed them that much, they'd all made him so proud. Shortly after that, he hung himself. No note, no explanation; just the words "Sorry Will" written on an old bible that was placed by his feet. Ed Keller died on a Monday, no family members held his trembling hand as he breathed his last breath, no burning building collapsed on him as he saved someone from certain death. No Ed Keller went out without a hero's goodbye, just quiet and alone, lost in a choice made in a loss of judgement.

"We've been planning it for weeks man, it's going to work," said the voice, purposely hushed as to not draw attention.

"I know we have, I just…," the hurried voice replied, drifting off and not finishing the thought.

"You gotta cut that negativity shit right out, or it won't work. That's how the thing works man."

"The thing," the hurried voice asked.

"Yes the thing. The universal truth thing," the hushed voice answered.

"Oh come on, don't start with that energy crap again."

"I'm telling you, the shit works okay?"

"That why we're in this predicament right now, because one of us willed it?"

"It doesn't work like that," the first voice replied.

"It doesn't hey, well that's mighty convenient. Works when you want it to then?"

"No, I…just….fuck sakes Turk. To hell with you. Be negative, see if I care."

"I will, thank you very much, Hanley the believer. Nice ring to it."

Turk and Hanley had signed the papers, they'd said the words the suits wanted them to say, but the hell if they were going to follow through and leave another man condemned for no solid reason. There was no way. The two men had both been ex-JTF2. It's where they'd met and formed the friendship they had now. It had been awhile since any of the two had used their skills in any manner other than to show off for some women at a bar but they'd both kept in tip top shape and regularly frequented a shooting range out of town to keep up their marksmanship.

Hanley had found out through an accomplice, a one Miss Wan that Will was being held in an old warehouse and with that information they were going to break William out. They had no idea if they stood a chance, but dying trying to do the right thing would be more than enough of a reward if it came to that. It would at least right their karma and that helped put Hanley's mind at ease, though he couldn't speak for Turk.

"Well tomorrow may very well be the last day of our lives and this here, tonight. It may be our last time to drink a nice cold whiskey," Hanley said, breaking the silence between the two.

"I think that deserves a toast of some sort. Mr. Clean Energy, you should do the speaking on this one," Turk added.

Hanley cleared this throat and tried to find the words; he had never had to address something like this before and after weeks of pretending this wasn't happening, they'd reached the precipice of a moment that couldn't be taken back once began.

"There hasn't been much I've done in my life that I can honestly say makes me proud of the man I have become. I've done things I'm not sure were the right thing to do, but orders from men who carried more pristine than me called for these things to be done. And they needed men who could get them done. That's us man. The guys who can do the things others can't. Though up until now, it's always been for hidden agendas and less than honest rewards. Tomorrow may be our redemption. We've been provided these skills, for a reason. For what? To play clean up for a paycheque? No. Maybe it was all for this moment. We don't know what Will is, maybe he's an alien, or maybe he's a step in evolution. Whatever he is, he shouldn't have survived that fall or the flame that came after, but he did. I can't help but think it's because he's meant to do something bigger. I can feel that. I think that's why you found him in that tub Turk. We play a part in this I know we do, I just know it. So here's to us man, here is to being part of the bigger picture. Here's to finally playing a part."

"Shit Hanley that was pretty good. I'll drink to that. To playing a part," Turk said as he raised his cup to Hanley's. The clink that followed sealed the moment, a pact amongst men who strived for a higher virtue. Maybe it was just a cheers to anyone else, but the "why" that was behind the cheers, meant something deeper.

# Derek S. Wruth

The two men sat and drank in a small concealed booth in a pub no one really went to. It was perhaps the biggest thing being planned in the city that night and no one batted an eye. To pretend we know all that happens in a place we claim to know seems to reek of dupable naivety.

The building that held Will was a 3 storey abandoned warehouse that, whoever they were, had come in taken over and established an operations centre out of. The security was tight; men on the roof and armed guards patrolled the perimeter on foot. It was going to be one hell of a rescue job, the two men were sure of that.

Turk had never thought he might die before 50; he was sheepish in the belief that he kind of thought he would live forever. The thought of what they were going to do this evening made him think the thought. The thought he never liked to entertain, that being he would never retire. He didn't think of retirement as something owed, rather than something earned. He'd worked hard all his life, this was the why aspect of that, the reason he did what he did. As the hours drew on, he became increasingly aware that he may miss out on the very thing he worked so hard for, but perhaps this new objective was to over shadow that. This truly meant something, maybe it was Hanley's speech, maybe it was his nerves, whatever it was though, kept Turk feeling….something. Something he couldn't quite place, something he hadn't felt in a while. It made him feel alive.

At eight o'clock that evening the two men boarded into a black cube van they had "borrowed" from a warehouse downtown. They saw this stint numerous times on television shows and picture movies, the old business van being inconspicuous. Hopefully it rang true.

They pulled within a couple blocks of the place to hash out the plan of attack. They were outnumbered, outgunned. All they had was the element of surprise. That was their ace in the hole.

"Okay, so this is it Hanley. Are you ready for this," Turk asked as they pulled into an empty parking lot outside an old Target.

"Am I ready to die to clear my conscious you mean," Hanley responded questioningly.

"How about dying for a friend," Turk bantered back. He'd heard the line on a movie, though in the moment he couldn't remember which.

"That I could do Turk. That I could do."

# Chapter Twelve

The sight of his house made Ben feel like he could breathe. He'd felt oddly off after reading the article about the blue hero lady and it left him with a tingling in his hands that he just couldn't quite shake. He had it in his mind that he was going to have a small dinner than take a walk in the park; after all it was one of his favorite pastimes. The smell of the earth helped him to relax and right now, he needed relaxing.

After getting home he quickly unpacked his bags, hopped a warm shower and then proceeded to grab a quick sandwich for supper as he headed out the door. He was more than eager to be alone with his thoughts, surrounded by trees he wouldn't have to chop down.

The cool air rushed over his face as he broke the plane from his house to the outer world, it was a nice change each time. The stillness tonight was deafening, the moonlight cast a silver light on the ground, and it all looked and felt fucking fantastic. God he loved the outdoors.

Ben's hands kept on with the weird tingling, and though it didn't cause any immediate pain, he felt increasingly aware that something was probably wrong with them. It felt now that the sensation was radiating up his arms now too. A quick web search indicated he more than likely was facing carpal tunnel, though he had to sift through the cancers it suggested he may have first. Given his line of work, it made sense. The carpal tunnel that is, not the cancer.

The leave enriched branches that hung over the path he now walked on, made Ben think he was entering a tunnel into a new world, one where he didn't have to hide, one that didn't judge him by his past. Perhaps that's why he took these walks, to escape; a yearning to be free.

A sudden sharp pain in his right shoulder brought Ben to his knees.

"What the hell," it made him cry out as it begun to pulse up and down his arm.

"WHAT IS THIS," he yelled as he gave his arm a shake, as if to wake it up when it fell asleep.

The path ahead of him tore into a spiral, rising out of the ground; it uprooted a small tree about 50 feet ahead of him.

Earthquake he thought.

Ben ran for an opening, away from potential falling trees.

He gave his arm another shake.

Suddenly he was flying through the air, landing on his face in a pile of raised earth.

"Ok what in the hell is happening?"

His arm felt less of the pulsing sensation he had been dealing with.

This wasn't an earthquake.

His left arm began to tingle.

"Oh no," Ben said as he watched his left arm begin to lightly glow.

"This definitely is no earthquake."

He extended his left arm out, like he just shoved a door open.

As he did that, the ground in front of him tore apart and flung forward.

Ben cried out in anguish.

His mind started to race, his arms started to burn. None of this made sense.

Home. Get home and hide.

Ben took off sprinting for his house, keeping his arms folded over his chest, too afraid to point them at anything.

He flew through his door like a bat out of hell. He wasn't sure what to do with himself but he knew he had to just stop. Just for a minute.

Inhale deep.

1…….2…….3…….4…….5…….6…….7…….8…….9……. and 10.

Exhale the bullshit.

Repeat.

Repeat.

Repeat.

Dammit. Repeat.

Repeat until the world makes sense.

It wasn't making sense.

The impending doom feeling took over, Ben's heart pounded out of his chest.

The world began to shrink, his living room walls closing in too fast for his liking.

He was on his back facing his ceiling, legs rested up on a wall; trying to catch his breath.

He'd faced this before, the panic attacks. Enough so that he was referred to a specialist, they had taught him to implore the use of tools they gave him when these moments came. In layman's terms, they had taught him how to breathe and take time to himself. Right now however, he couldn't slow down.

Repeat.

Repeat.

Repeat.

Repea…..the world faded out.

A few hours later Ben woke up on his floor, on his side, face full of couch legs.

His head was killing him. His arms….weren't, they actually felt pretty good; that was interesting.

Ben got to his feet, he was a little shaken up but none the worse for wear. But now what?

What the hell had just happened? Would it happen again?

Ben's mind raced for answers and he had no idea where to get them.

His door caught his eye. It was still wide open.

He'd come in so fast he didn't think to close it properly.

The cool breeze crept in, luring him towards the night air.

Ben walked towards the opening.

He poked his head out, afraid to see something.

Though he didn't know what he expected to see, he after all; at least in this instance, was the monster.

Screw it.

Ben walked out, towards the tree tunnel, down the path to the opening.

The torn earth left by him was fairly obvious. Though maybe it could be mistaken for someone off-roading where they shouldn't be.

Ben walked to a part of the small meadow that was untouched by his hand.

He raised his palm upwards, like he was getting a palm reading.

He lifted it up.

As he did that, the ground in front of him tore and rose up, in a column like shape.

He tried the same thing with the other hand.

Same result. A column pitched forth out of the ground, reaching for the sky above.

What about the same time he wondered?

So he tried both hands this time.

A wave of earth tore upwards making a hell of a noise, and the sudden jerking movement under his feet put Ben on his ass.

"Shit," was the only word Ben could muster.

"What the hell is this," Ben asked aloud.

"Why is this happening to me?"

Suddenly an idea rushed through Ben's brain.

He knew what to do.

It was 12:00am on a Sunday night and here was Ben, hiding behind an old refrigerator.

This is what his life had come to. His friends would be so proud.

The old building smelled funny, it smelled funnier yet as Ben proceeded with the plan.

Just before 12:30am Ben had made the call.

Now he waited.

Ben had to piss. Dammit.

A noise downstairs made it worse.

Footsteps.

Faster.

Closer.

Ben's stomach began to hurt slightly.

What the hell?

Footsteps still.

Almost right outside.

Then a silence.

Suddenly the door flew open across the room, bouncing off a wall.

Ben couldn't quite grasp what he was seeing.

He stepped out from his hiding place slowly, his plan had worked.

As he got within earshot Ben spoke slowly; hoping not to startle.

"Took you long enough….hero."

# Chapter Thirteen

Eiri felt different. And not just because of what had happened. He felt…connected. Like something inside was finally waking up after being at rest for a long time; something familiar, something hiding.

He had managed to go south of the city to his favorite secluded highway. He drove it west, not very far, until he saw signs for the campground, those same signs also pointed out that there was a gas station a little further down the road. All in all it seemed like the perfect spot to lay low.

Driving into the site he saw no booth taking camping fares, no signs of foot traffic or signs of car traffic of any great volume. An old car did sit in a small parking lot, but it was probably just a day visitor. There was no one in it or standing around it he noticed as he drove by slowly. No car seats inside meant no children, a bumper sticker saying something about being on the path indicated it was probably someone religious, maybe they were out praying or something. Eiri didn't feel threatened by it, so he continued on.

As he drove farther down the trail made for small vehicles, the shimmering blue lake lay to his right, surrounded by trees and hills. Save for what looked like a communications tower across the lake, the place looked pretty secluded and it was precisely where Eiri needed to be right now. He had to figure out what was happening, he had to do some trial runs. But first he needed to sleep. Eiri found a level spot off a ways through the trees to set up camp and then he went straight into his sleeping bag. When he fell into a sleep, he dreamed weird dreams.

Eiri waited until the morning sun began to rise before he attempted any funny business. Yes the place was secluded but he figured why test it and then be recorded by a damn jogger or something. He had to be careful. He knew that much.

Okay. Now how the hell does this work? Eiri hadn't a clue.

He stuck his arm out and extended his fingers.

And nothing happened.

Okay....so then maybe he thought if he just...

Eiri twisted his arm out this time....and still nothing happened.

What the hell....Eiri knew this was real, he knew he was awake when it happened and definitely not dreaming.....right?

Eiri tried extending both arms out this time, palms up and raised them.

Nothing happened yet again.

Come on Eiri. You gotta figure this out. Somehow it happens, there's something you're missing. Okay so got to think back. Both times what was happening? Greg. Well it couldn't be just him being there, god that'd be useless. He pissed Eiri off by just thinking of him. Wait a minute.

That's it. Eiri was mad both times. Okay. Get angry. Just think of Greg, that should do it.

He felt the back of his neck heat up, a sure fire sign that the rage was coming on. His fists balled tightly and his breathing began to speed up. His arms began to tremble and they also began to burn but inside. Okay so that's different but somehow...not entirely.

Eiri imagined Greg standing by a nearby tree, smoking a cigarette for whatever reason, just going about his business.

Then he imagined the rock off to his right lifting off the ground, separating from the earth where it sat. Eiri made the motion with his hands, he imagined it rising from the ground, tearing the earth it was situated in, he motioned his arms quickly towards the imaginary Greg as if he was throwing him a ball to catch. And as he completed the movement, the tree that stood there exploded into flying bark as the small boulder bounced off it and rolled into the bushes behind.

Eiri spent the rest of the morning in the forest testing his ability with various objects he could move. He came to an understanding that if he upped his rage he could move larger objects like boulders or uproot fully grown trees. Though he tried not to disturb too much of the natural habit, after all he cared deeply for the nature around him.

Nature didn't judge him for being him, it never called him names or bullied him because he was different and most importantly, nature never left. Eiri never really felt like he connected to much in this world but the feeling he got deep in the forest, it resonated on another level with him and he knew to protect that feeling.

Eiri had been practicing his craft for a few days when a morning came that he heard loud splashing sounds off in the distance. He had decided he needed to investigate the source of these noises; after all they threatened his sanctuary. No one else was out here and the sound was too big to come from a fish.

The forest floor was difficult to navigate quietly but Eiri had grown accustomed on how to step, where to walk and where to avoid when it came to sneaking in the trees. He slowly made his way to the waterfront in hopes he could see what made such a ruckus. The noise was still ongoing, albeit quieter from before. As Eiri broke through the trees and onto the rocky beach, a feeling hit him in the gut.

Eiri found himself on one knee, clutching at his abdomen when he finally regained his composure. He looked up and around. It was quiet all around now and the water lay still and tranquil. He had missed it.

The birds woke Eiri most mornings now. He never really bothered to check the time because it didn't really matter out here. No television. No cellphones. No screens. It was tranquil, the kind of thing he needed right now to quell the constant barrage of fear in his own mind. Fear of failure, fear of people, fear and self-doubt. He'd read once that the two things that hold most people back from becoming successful is fear and self-doubt. Eiri had a plan and to make the plan work he had to first work on himself. So he began meditating every morning down by the lake to calm the noises inside his head. It helped him work out what was going on with him and it allowed him to be more present. After all his own emotions being out of touch was what drove him out here, into self-exile and that just wouldn't do for Eiri. Eiri had a plan.

As he sat in the sand and listened to the water flowing back and forth, reaching onto the land as if it were trying to crawl out, Eiri closed his eyes and breathed in deeply. He held his breath and exhaled slowly and as he did so he repeated the word "Serenity". It was his mantra. Eiri found it difficult to just sit there and not have his mind race off to a thousand different thoughts. But if he pictured the word and repeated it, it helped silence the noise. Serenity.

# Chapter Fourteen

47 seconds. That was the perfect amount of time to warm up a cold cup of coffee in the microwave. Without cream or sugar of course, because they blended together better after. Grant Thomas knew this because Grant Thomas had been warming up cups of coffee since just after Ben was born. Any parent would know what that was like, at least the coffee drinking parents would. Microwaveable; another interesting fact for you, not all containers are microwaveable. Grant found this out the hard way and the unfortunate blunder had cost him his microwave and his favorite soup container, it was a rough day.

Once his cup was closer to the temperature more to his liking, Grant opened the door to his camper and stepped outside into the early morning air. It never ceased to change how it made him feel when that cool breeze hit him; it invigorated and relaxed him all at the same time. Keeping to a routine also kept the dreams at bay and that quite literally helped Grant sleep at night.

The dreams, more like nightmares than anything remotely related to a dream. Grant had thought it over quite a bit before deciding that those dreams were related to that house and that selling it to rough it out at a lake in a camper sounded like his best bet. So here he was in a lawn chair at a secluded spot a little ways south of the city. It wasn't totally off the grid; there were some stores down the highway, so Grant could keep pretty well supplied as he made his stay. And more often than not nowadays when Grant slept he did not see the ships or the creatures anymore. He didn't hear the explosions or the grinding of fallen metal framing of skyscrapers collapsing under piles of dust and rubble; he didn't hear the gun shots or the shouts of people, their screams. In one particular dream he saw a bridge flying, it almost felt familiar, and it ended up falling onto a crowded street full of people. Then gunshots began and Grant was teleported to a busy road. There were people running and yelling and there were loud bangs of falling glass. Then there was a man and he was floating by, and there was someone else. Three people in total, all brought ruin to this scene, it was madness. Grant could do nothing but watch. That same dream repeated itself almost nightly for months before Grant moved out. It was beginning to be too much for him and the whiskey quit working the way it was supposed to work. So here Grant was, roughing it.

About midway through the egg sandwich he'd prepared for this beautiful morning, Grant heard the noise again. It was the same noise he had heard the other day. Something in the far off trees was making some snapping noises. Breaking branches maybe? Grant couldn't quite tell but he knew he had to find out. It sounded a little ways away but walkable he thought since he could hear it.

As far as Grant could tell the sound came from the east, deeper into the wooded area around the south portion of the lake. Grant hadn't really explored that part of the trees yet so he didn't know quite what to expect, he only hoped he could be quiet enough to sneak up on the noise maker. He'd just have to watch his step. Grant could do that.

After walking for a few minutes Grant saw what looked like a small creek coming up through the trees. He rather wished he had known about this particular creek when he decided to practice. Though admittedly the lake did challenge Grant, for there was more of it. Grant had just figured a way to traverse the rocks to cross the small body of water when a strange feeling hit him, the same one as the other day when he was practicing. This one felt a lot more manageable though, it didn't bring him to his knees in the trees with that feeling of helpless to the nausea that came with it. No this was about a tenth of that, it made Grant's stomach feel fluttery but not like he had to throw up, like something was coming and it was a good thing.

*Solace Rises*

The loud crash of something large hitting the trees behind Grant brought him out of the feeling. Grant felt the hostility behind that noise and ran for cover behind a tree. Suddenly a large boulder bounced off something and rolled by Grant into the forest, whatever it was out there was throwing boulders. Grant for a minute thought he'd slept in and this was just the weird dreams returning when his cover splintered behind him and a pain wedged through his upper back. The pain dug into him like something he'd never experienced, it radiated down his back and caused Grant's eyes to water. Grant had to keep moving. Instinctively as Grant went for more cover he threw his hands up towards the creek and water flew upwards. Through the loud splashing noise of water hitting forest and rock Grant heard a sudden yell. It worked! Grant used the time to run.

Grant wasn't at all stealthy on this run through the woods. He fell and crashed and made no heed to the loud noises that he was making. Grant realised with the yell he heard that whoever it was, was indeed a "who" and not a "what". This brought a little relief to Grant. He had no idea where he would go; he sure didn't want to lead the pursuer to his home. If Grant drew him to the water of the lake however, Grant could surprise him again with some offense.

As Grant ran he noted that if he glanced to his right he could see the lake through the treeline. He thought that if he could find a place to hide in the treeline and draw the attacker to the lake with a distraction he could surprise them from his hiding place. To what ends Grant did not know, he had never faced something like this before, it felt an awful lot like kill or be killed though.

~

Eiri was ready. He'd set the trap making excess sounds in the woods to draw in whoever was making those water noises. They would come from the west, that's where the splashing had come from, so it made sense to Eiri to expect them from there. Eiri would be ready for them when they appeared.

Eiri took his place by a small creek with boulders in and around it; at least Eiri had something to fight back with if he was attacked. He waited patiently, as he had been doing. He knew someone would find him eventually, Eiri hadn't really intended to but he was pretty sure he'd killed the men who attacked him in the city. That action had to come with repercussions. If this was them well Eiri wouldn't go down without a fight.

Suddenly a man appeared through the trees, walking along carefully, as if he was hunting. Eiri ignored the pain in his abdomen and kept his focus on the approaching man. As the stranger got closer, Eiri made the split second decision to go on the offensive. He reached out for a boulder sitting a few feet to his left and hurled it at the man.

The throw wasn't Eiri's best attempt and the rock sailed far off to the right of the hunter instead. Eiri then proceeded to throw another one, it was slightly askew and hit a tree before rolling into the forest. The man had ducked behind a tree for cover so Eiri picked up the biggest rock he could see around him and threw it for the tree.

CRACK!

This time the boulder had found its mark and the tree which the man hid behind splintered into a hundred chunks of wooden shrapnel and toppled over in a loud crash. A yell sounded out and Eiri knew he'd done some sort of damage so he decided to capitalize and go towards the stranger to see if he was incapacitated enough for a final blow. He just had to cross the creek and finish this. Eiri had gotten about halfway when the creek hit him in the gut.

The water hitting Eiri was a surprise but the fact it hit him hard enough to send him back across the creek and into the trees was what really got Eiri's attention. It had to have come from the man, this meant Eiri wasn't the only one who was…well who was like this. Eiri had to know more about the stranger.

Tracking the man through the trees was no problem, he wasn't being very quiet. Eiri guessed he was about 100-150 feet ahead of him, judging by the noise he was making. So maybe the guy wasn't a professional, maybe he wasn't hunting Eiri, but Eiri knew nothing for sure until he spoke with him. The sudden quiet stopped Eiri in his tracks, where'd he go? The water. He would go for the water, I mean with that power why not, after all that was probably his best chance against Eiri.

Eiri crept out of the treeline when he heard a splash, he stepped eagerly forward waiting for the attack. A quick look around and Eiri realised he didn't have much to throw at the man, but he was rather hoping they could talk instead of killing each other. No one stood by the lake or hunkered by the water ready to fight Eiri. The shoreline was empty. It was a trap.

The splashing noise came from behind Eiri, like a waterfall had just appeared and started dumping water. Eiri turned around as quick as he could, closed his eyes and braced for an impact by bringing up his forearms together to form a makeshift shield in front of himself. After another loud splashing noise followed up by a couple drops of water hitting his face, Eiri opened his eyes and saw the torn ground floating in front of him like a wall.

"Stop whoever you are, just wait," Eiri called out.
"So you can throw another boulder at me?! Yeah right asshole."
"Can't you see? I'm just like you!"

~

Grant watched as the man dropped the makeshift shield made of earth down and put his hands up. Without the shield the two stood across from each other now. Grant felt like an animal, his breath was heavy, his eyes wide and focused. The stranger looked calm for some reason, no eyes widened, no heavy breathing, he just stood there and then he smiled at Grant.

# Chapter Fifteen

"Well what do we do with him?"

"We keep him where he is, he ain't goin nowhere."

"The cells are supposed to be built to withstand them so yeah, he shouldn't be goin anywhere."

"Good cause we're going out tonight. Got another tip on the dynamic duo out there and now it's time I ask them some questions. We'll leave a handful of stationary guards just in case but we need all boots on the ground for this one. After all there are two of them."

"Bringing them where? Here? What makes you think they'll cooperate?"

"I said I had some questions not the Bureau. They say shoot on sight."

"This won't be another incident like New Mexico."

---

Hanley was readying his demolitions bag when the alarm went off from within the makeshift compound of whatever black suit shady organization this was. This was followed by a mass exodus of what appeared to be a small army of people in black military garb loading up and shipping out in a hurry.

"Uhh Turk?"

"Yeah I see it I just don't understand why."

It didn't take very long before the alarm went silent and a whole convoy of black trucks were gone off the premise.

"So do we go knock then Turk?"

"Hell yeah we do, no time better than right now."

The unexpected knock on the back door of their van had Turk and Hanley instantaneously point both their barrels in that direction. They looked at each other and nodded.

Suddenly the door opened and before the men could react at all, the front of the van lifted and they were propelled headfirst ass over tea kettle out the back doors.

"We aren't here to hurt you, we are here to help but those guns make a person awfully nervous gentlemen."

Turk could not believe what he was seeing. It was that crazy lady from the news.

"Who the hell are you and what the hell do you want," Turk asked her forthright. His gun had fallen out of reach and he was still having a hard time understanding just what the hell was happening.

"You only need to understand that we are both here to help you and that we both have a mutual friend in Miss Wan."

Turk glanced over to Hanley for some reassurance. The woman's friend that she showed up with was helping him up off the ground and with that Turk followed suit and reached his hand out to the woman.

"Name's Turk, that's Hanley."

"My name is Ben, can't speak for her though. Call her hero."

"Don't call me that for god's sake. Name is Ev."

"Alright then Ben and Ev. That you guys with the alarm trick?"

"You're welcome," Ben replied through a smirk.

"That was totally my idea."

Evelyn scoped out the building as the men exchanged pleasantries. She wondered what these two guys had planned to get into this place.

"Were you guys just going to walk up to the front door and knock or did you have a plan," she asked.

Hanley held up his bag and opened it to show the duo what was inside.

"So a really big knock then. That would have drawn them to one side or the other and allow for a small window. Hmm not bad," Ev said out loud in reply. She scanned the area for options. For a plan.

"Almost wish we would have waited to see that go down. You two look the John Mclean type," Ben added.

"So gentlemen as we have been standing here I've come up with a plan. Sketchy building, bad guy type lair feel to it. I'm betting where they're holding Will is towards the rear, like most dungeons and stuff am I right," Ev explained rather animatedly to the group. She walked along the outer fence, which was made out of solid concrete. She had to go through it, it was as simple as that. Okay Evelyn she thought to herself, this should be just like doing it with the trees. Just a push.

"Hey it doesn't matter where the explosive goes, as long as...."

Evelyn didn't let him finish his sentence. Instead she raised her hand and pushed a portion of the wall in on itself so it broke and flew backwards into the warehouse. The faces of the two were precisely why she loved doing what she did. They were surprised and Evelyn knew that was not going to get old for her anytime soon.

"That's going to bring some attention, it wasn't exactly subtle," said Turk as he looked in through the hole that was now in the solid wall.

"Can one of you keep six here in case someone shows up? Me and Ev are going to go round back and see what that side of the building looks like, maybe we'll get lucky and find a door unlocked."

"Yeah I got this. Turk you go with them and keep me posted."

"You got it man. Head on a swivel hey bro...."

The first shot rang through the air just as it pierced through Hanley's right eye. The second shot hit him in the chest.

Turk didn't even hear it before his best friend and lifelong mentor was dead in his arms.

"What was...

"Turk get down!"

The ground in front of the trio made a loud crunching sound and it rose to form a wall in front of them.

"Ev that won't hold for too long, what's the plan?"

Evelyn had never been under gunfire nor in any way this close to a firearm being expelled, especially towards her. She began to freeze up and her legs began shaking. Come on Evelyn. Be the hero. Just like the books you read or the books you write. You can do this. Think.

The gunfire was coming from one of the windows just above them somewhere and if Evelyn could just pinpoint where, she may be able to take out that portion of the wall and have them fall.

Turk began returning fire after the initial shock of what just happened started to subside. It didn't take much before Turk had hit the sniper in the chest and dropped him.

"Think there's much more? It's hard to see all the way up like that so I can't get good shots in. I want to make sure all of these sons of bitches get it."

"Okay follow me. We'll go round back and get in there; maybe there'll be better vantage points for you inside."

Evelyn led the group around the back of the large building and as she turned the corner she saw a door. Her whole body was shaking and she couldn't control it, she just had to stop for a minute. Someone just died in front of her and that made all this so real now, it was the second death she had been close to in a few weeks.

"Do we go through there Ev? It'll probably be a lot quieter then blowing through another wall again or maybe I can raise us up to the windows and we can go through that way, at least they wouldn't expect that."

Evelyn didn't know what to do, she didn't know whether to go right or left or up or down. She just caused the death of a man and she wasn't sure how to feel about that, it was all getting so real so fast. Not now Evelyn, you can beat yourself up when you tell Candy about what you've been up to with all these late nights, but right now you got to hold it together. The voice in her head gave her damn good advice sometimes when she chose to entertain it that is.

"We take the dam door. Get ready because I'm going to knock really loudly."

The burning sensation began in Evelyn's upper shoulders, it quickly radiated down her arms and felt like it was going to explode out of her fingertips. She walked up to the door to knock a few times then she took a few steps back. Ev raised her palms up and pushed as hard as she possibly could towards the door.

~

"Get me Nadia. She'll want to hear this. Ma'am they're here right now. They've already taken out Thompson and part of this west side wall. I don't know where they are now but I'm sure… Wait there's something happening towards the rear door. I think they're knocking. Ma'am should…"

The line went dead before Nadia heard the end of that sentence.

"Turn this dam thing around, they got us."

~

The door and most of the wall surrounding it flew inwards with such force that it took out supports and catwalks from the upper level. Dust and debris covered the immediate area and the group took cover on opposite sides of the huge hole. When the dust settled over the silence and the group regained a bit of visual into the building, Evelyn saw the body. Somebody had been approaching the door on the other side.

"I'm going in and taking the right side. If anything moves I'll kill it."

Turk slowly took a look around the corner favoring the right of what was once a door. A hidden glance allowed him to catch sight of two people moving quietly but not fully covertly throughout the warehouse. One was up on a catwalk that seemed to run around the place and one on the ground, both were hiding towards the east wall.

There also seemed to be a room off in the back. Will was probably in there, Turk could feel it.

"So there are two that I can see and they're both on the opposite wall. One is up on a catwalk behind a couple of barrels and one is on the ground level stashed out behind a couple boxes. Not sure they know what exactly they're in for so let's give em hell, for Hanley."

This time Ben followed Turk in and his adrenaline must have kicked in because it felt like slow motion when they breached the hole and entered the warehouse. Turk shot towards the catwalk barrels shortly upon entering; he then quickly took cover and kept up the barrage. Ben snuck quickly towards the boxes Turk had mentioned that the second guy was hiding behind. He took a breath and pictured what had to be done. He would have to dig deep down and lift the ground below the concrete floor that this place sat on. As he opened his eyes Evelyn stepped in front of him and blew the boxes through the wall and all. The hiding man was definitely gone now.

"Hey Ev I had…"

Evelyn had put a hand on his shoulder before he finished his sentence and something in her eyes made him listen.

"Less blood on your hands," was all she had to say.

"That bastard on the catwalk was a slick one but I got him though, we good to find our boy? Haven't seen any more movement other than those two so perhaps this is our window," Turk whispered as he crept up to Ev and Ben.

An illuminated room behind a solid door stood alone in the corner. It looked unnatural for the architecture and surrounding structure. That meant someone had built that thing. Will had to be in there.

"He's here," Ben announced as he took a look through the small window on the door.

"Okay so how do we…"

Evelyn hit the wall with all she had. It did nothing.

"I'm decent when it comes to unlocking doors. Hanley was the guy but I paid attention. Let me try."

With a loud release of air the large door opened and silence took the warehouse.

"Turk?"

The voice came from a darkened corner in the enforced room.

"We got you, let's get you somewhere safe man," Turk said as he half walked half ran up to William. When they got Will to the light the group could see that although he'd fallen through a flaming building and had been kidnapped and held hostage, he looked to be in relatively good shape.

Evelyn walked up to Will and took a look at him. He instinctively tried to hide himself, but Evelyn got through.

"Hey we're like you," Evelyn gestured to both Ben and herself, "you're not alone anymore."

William began to cry.

# Chapter Sixteen

William remembered the fall. It was hotter than hell and it felt like it lasted forever. The inferno that overtook him and Wesley was a temperature that William couldn't describe in words. It dried his eyes out and regressed his bunker gear to an overpriced snowsuit; it just couldn't hold back the flame. William closed his eyes and waited for it to end when a sudden stop of his fiery descent meant that he'd probably hit the ground floor. A quick glance to his right showed that there wasn't much left of his good friend James Wesley. Wait why was William still alive? They'd fallen into the same fire, why was Will not burned to ashes? Before he could register what was actually happening to him Will began to run, through smoke and flame, through dust and ash. He ran as far back into the building as he could and into an abandoned apartment, flame still surrounded him and yet he remained unscathed by its brutal licks. He didn't truly want to survive this, he had no idea what was wrong with him and he thought it better that the world didn't know either. So he found a spot and he hid, for as long as he could in the dark. Hours passed and Will didn't sleep or rest, instead he lay staring at the porcelain side of a bath tub wondering what he was and what they would do to him. A shuffling noise of movement meant the gig was up and there was no more hiding, he only hoped they killed him quickly. For a second Will thought he heard a familiar voice through the wreckage.

"Turk?"

When she slept she dreamt of things she had never dreamt of before. She saw skulls for heads on regular humans, eyes of black and misshapen limbs. Everybody looked so broken, so deadened. Her latest foray into the dreamscape of freaking nightmares included seeing the city she grew up in torn down and reduced to dust and ash. Deadened people took over the streets, screaming and crying as though lost in a sea of death. One lady even took the time out of her ever so busy dream life and came right up to Evelyn, grabbed her shoulders and she spoke, "don't trust him."

"How's Will? He ready?"

"Ev. You know he isn't, he can barely talk."

"Well we can't stay here, they could have followed us, we got to keep moving."

"Yeah? To where? It's been days and he's still out there patrolling. How far can we get?"

"Far enough from here, that maybe his memory lets us go. I dunno but it's worth a shot isn't it?"

"It's not like there's a ton of us left, but if we could bypass him, we might at least stand a chance.

The group slowly and silently moved towards the back of their makeshift compound. The hole in the roof told Evelyn that someone had found them....recently. As long as they stuck to the shadows and avoided open areas, Evelyn felt confident that they could make it across the city. They moved and they moved carefully. Slow. Steady. Slow. Steady.

The loud cracking sound and the flash that followed signalled Evelyn that he had found them.

"Evy!"

"I smell you....and there's no more running."

Evelyn woke up in a pile of sweat and instantaneously felt the residual pain of grinding her teeth.

"Oh for.... sakes."

Evelyn fell back asleep shortly and this time she didn't dream. Though truth be told, she feared the dreams, often she feared sleeping at all. It made her feel vulnerable and exposed, like a damn nerve that didn't heal right, she couldn't stand it and she definitely couldn't understand it either. The less she thought of it, the less it drove her mad.

"Hey Ev, he's awake, if you want to talk to him."

Evelyn woke with a jolt. She glanced over to her nightstand, her photograph rested against her lamp. She was in the now.

"Thanks Ben, I'll be right down."

Evelyn knew the importance of this talk, because she knew he was another one of them. In the last two months he was the third and Ev had to know why and now she understood she had to get him to talk. She didn't not like the guy but she wasn't sure and she had to be careful. After all, she did understand the stakes.

As she brushed her teeth she wondered who he was. Why all her dreams were suddenly so lucid and terrifying escaped her, again maybe what she had been doing was attributing to her changing psyche. A few months ago she was just an author and a bit of an introvert and now she could hurl concrete fences into walls and she was going against bad guys with guns. A part of her thought she maybe died in that car accident and this was her mind coping. It all seemed too crazy. Like one of her books.

"So are we going to talk about the other night?" Evelyn had been avoiding that very question since they got back from rescuing Will and right now she wasn't even sure she knew how to talk about it? "Ev I'm being honest, some real serious stuff went down out there and I'm wondering how that is affecting you. It wouldn't be wrong if it did ya know. I'm here to talk if you need."

"Ben I know. I get it, I do and thank you but right now I just have to process some things okay? Words won't fix this right now I just have to feel it." Ben let out a silenced sigh of disappointment and turned back for the other rooms. Evelyn knew that probably wasn't handled the best way but she wasn't looking to fix it right now for she had other pressing matters.

"Hey where is Turk at? I should probably talk to him." Ben slowed down. Internally he debated on telling her off, he couldn't figure her out and it aggravated him. He just wanted to understand. After all he had thrown his all into the ring, belief and all. He needed to see this all through. He just had to.

"He's in the kitchen."

Why were the lights in this place colored like those of a hospital? They even gave off the slightest buzzing noise if you listened carefully enough, Turk was always listening carefully.

"Hey uh Turk is it?"

"Hero."

Evelyn half laughed, "yeah something like that. Listen, how are you? Things got pretty rough out there."

"Yeah no I was in the service, I get what's on the line and I've been in contact with his next of kin. Unfortunately this kind of shit happens."

Ev felt a little taken aback at what almost seemed like apathy but she was assured could not have been. The man was merely sure of what had to be done and he got it done and she got that.

"Okay cool I just thought I'd ask."

Turk wasn't about to let this stranger know what he was feeling. It wasn't any of her business and besides he felt it out at appropriate times.

"No harm no foul. So what's next?"

Evelyn hadn't thought about that. Now that they were at where they were at, what were they supposed to do? She hadn't a clue.

"We're working on that Turk. You'll know soon enough."

~

"Do it again, but this time without the doubt."

"I'm not…"

"I feel you, don't doubt me now."

"Okay. No doubt."

The water by the lakeshore rose up, it swirled around and shot straight out towards the opposite shoreline only to bend back up and slam into the surface.

"How was that for doubting?"

"Better Grant, but we still have lots to do before we go back."

Just then a large rock shot up into the air and spun around. It spun faster and faster until it became a loud whirring sound.

"Eir it's getting late, we can't be too loud."

The rock then shot across the surface of the lake as if a giant skipped his favorite pebble. It flew into the trees on the opposite shore.

"Eiri!"

"Relax old man, I scouted it earlier while you slept in. No one's here."

"Christ sakes kid. Did you meditate yet?"

"Not yet, was waiting for your old bones to join, besides the sun is just rising. Perfect time."

The pair meditated most mornings, it was something Eiri had begun doing quite some time ago though not as much as he did now. The peace it helped bring aided the pair as they explored their abilities. They both knew it would take some time and they knew better than to rush it and to do that the two agreed they needed to acquire a little more patience. Meditation was the happy medium for them both.

"I got to run into town at some point today I got uh old man stuff to pick up."

"Sounds good Grant. Grab me some Pepsi while you're there, I'm running low."

"Sure thing Eir, sure thing."

# Chapter Seventeen

**Three Years Later**

"I don't know what to tell you, he said ten guys max. This is a whole different level than ten guys max."

"I don't see the other choice. We have to go in because for all we know those girls could still be alive."

"She's right you know, we're already here, no authorities are getting here for another fifteen to twenty minutes. These guys can pack up and leave by then with no trace. If there is any chance that they could get away with this then we have to stop them."

Evelyn knew in her heart the girls in the basement were still there, she felt them and she had to act on that.

"Ben you go down but go slow and we'll meet you down there. Me and Will are going to storm the top floor."

"Sounds good Ev. Give these bastards hell."

Evelyn and Will crept up a set of stairs that led into the top floor off a balcony. They could hear muffled voices as they drew closer to the landing and Evelyn knew what she had to do, they'd planned for this.

The Molotov secured in her bag hadn't leaked much but enough that Evelyn decided the whole bag could go, she didn't want it back and so she readied it.

"Light it up Will," she said as she lit the cloth protruding out of the bottle and tossed it through the open door where the voices hid.

The next few minutes Evelyn crouched down and shielded her eyes. When Will needed her he would let her know. Screams filled the air and she knew Will was hitting his marks, it sounded horrible.

"Basement time, they're toast."

Evelyn could tell by the silence through the flames that Will had indeed dealt with them.

When the duo got to the basement level they could tell they'd just missed a firefight.

"Ben!"

"Eh Benjamin where you at man," Will shouted repeatedly through the hazing smoke.

A loud clanging noise of what sounded like metal hitting metal rang through the basement.

"Follow that sound Will."

At the source of the sound was Ben desperately trying to unlock a padlock that held a bevy of women behind cold locked bars.

"Hey let me give it a try," said Evelyn as she approached. She'd blown locks to bits before.

She motioned for the girls to back up and they did. She raised her hand and then with a motion blew the lock clear off the cell door.

"We have to get out of here now."

As the group got the rest of the girls out of the building, they could hear sirens in the distance getting closer. As they did most nights when law enforcement were arriving, the group vanished.

~

The hooded figure watched from afar but close enough to see. They studied the group as they went about their duties, unknowingly being surveillanced for greater purposes. The figure watched intently once realising that perhaps this group could do it, because according to the book, they would have to. So the hooded figure watched intently. Two still remained unaccounted for but the figure knew they would show up sooner or later. So the figure watched intently.

~

"Too much petrol."

"I'm sorry what?"

"Your molotov trick. There was too much gas in the bottle so the fire burned too hot too quick, it could have spread too fast for me to control. Maybe less gas next time."

"You okay Will?"

"All good chief, just an idea is all."

"Much appreciated. Hey I've got word on those mercenaries we were talking about. I'll send it to you yeah?"

"Yes ma'am I would definitely love to look at that. I think I know one of the guys."

Evelyn walked through the compound as she cleared her head. God she missed the sun, hunkering down below ground killed her some days. Today was one of those days.

"Hey Ev I got good news come see this."

"What you got for me Shorty?"

"There are reports of something happening in china town. An assault of some kind but the call got cut off so I'm not really sure what's happening."

"I'll take Ben and go check it out. No biggie."

"Actually Ben just asked for the day off, he isn't feeling too good. You're going to have to go with Will."

"Alright cool, I'll go find him."

China town wasn't the friendliest place to frequent, they had heard lots of stories of mob bosses and the sort criminalizing the streets in and surrounding the square. Evelyn had heard about these kinds of things on movies and what not but to come to find there was some truth behind it made her feel uneasy. Hidden in broad daylight truths always made her uneasy, as they should anyone.

"Ev. You read me?"

"Loud and clear Shorty what do you got for me?"

"Call came in from the address coming to your phone. Guy seemed distraught and he spoke of powered people. Yeah that's right, maybe y'all ain't as unique as you think."

"We'll see about that. We're coming up on the place. Going silent til we know what's going on."

After driving for a bit Will gestured to the building in front of them. At first glance the place looked like an old post office or something. She stood old and stone, as did much aged architecture in the old parts of the city.

"That's her. I'll pull round back and find somewhere to park."

As Will cornered the street he couldn't help but to feel that something wasn't quite right. Why was it so quiet? Where were the sirens?

"There. The bay door, I can get us through there."

"Okay Ev. Hey did you bring the non-lethals?"

"Does a bear go in the woods? Check the black bag on the third shelf."

Once they had parked, the duo understood they only had so much time before law enforcement showed up. There was no time for messing this up.

Evelyn quickly cased out the bay door before she blew it clear off its hinges and into the garage it was attached to.

"After you good sir."

"Always the lady," Will replied as he snuck into the building.

The place looked like it had been abandoned for a long while before they broke in. Everything was absolutely blanketed in old dust. Some lights were still on but they flowed dimly and barely illuminated anything.

"Okay what the f…."

"Will, come here. Look at this."

Ev had taken a knee towards a railed balcony by some old stairs. She was pointing at the ground.

"Footsteps. Son of a bitch."

"Yup. Should we follow them? I bet they lead somewhere exciting!"

"Yes Ev we should follow them. Guns ready yeah?"

"Always."

The tracks didn't really lead anywhere. Will followed them carefully and in the middle of a room they just stopped. Disappeared just like that.

After a short discussion and a minor disagreement the pair did come to the conclusion that the tracks had in fact just disappeared and bad tracking wasn't the case.

"So what do we do now Ev? We're in open water here now."

Before either of the two could utter another word a huge force pushed them over the railing and down a one storey drop onto a wooden dust covered floor.

"What the he…"

Before Will finished his sentence Evelyn caught a brief glimpse of movement on the floor they were just on. With all she had left she raised her arms and pushed outwards. The floor above them splintered violently upwards into a million pieces and a sudden yell echoed out. Evelyn knew she had to move. Where was Will? There was dust everywhere with the collapse.

"Ugh."

"Will follow my voice where are you? We gotta move."

Suddenly all the lights went out and as dark as the place had been it got even darker. In the darkness came loud crashing noises like things were being thrown about and smashed everywhere. Evelyn hadn't felt this scared in a long time. A sudden silence filled the building. Evelyn felt herself being lifted off the ground and abruptly dropped onto her back. She felt terrified.

"Hey Ev, do you have the lighter?"

Evelyn searched her pockets until she felt it.

"Yes, here I'll slide it to you."

"Just light it. We can't risk losing it and we have to get the hell out of here."

Evelyn fumbled the lighter in her pocket and once she got it upright she looked to where Will's voice came from, "give 'em hell."

Will gave it everything he had and he meant absolutely everything because the small flame of the lighter turned into a massive firestorm that swirled into the upper floors. Whoever was up there definitely got one hell of a surprise. Stifled yells and loud footsteps made Evelyn realise this was their window.

"Will grab my arm we're moving."

They half ran half fell through the dust and down a scattered hallway towards a door lined by sunlight. As they broke the threshold into the fresh air of the alley, Evelyn knew they weren't quite out of the woods yet.

"The van Will and then we'll be home free. We gotta hurry!"

A loud clanging noise of angered metal came from their left and when Evelyn glanced towards the sound she saw a large garbage can coming right at them. In a split second reaction she stuck out her arms and pushed the can back into the wall. It hit the wall with a large crash, toppled sideways and slid down the alley away from them.

No further encounters happened as the duo reached the van and sped off. And as they drove away Evelyn watched out the rear window in case anyone was to follow.

"Hey Will?"

"Yeah Ev?"

"We're not alone are we?"

"Doesn't look like it anymore. What we gonna do about it?"

Evelyn wasn't sure yet but she understood she had to think of something, there were people depending on her insight and guidance. This was too important to freeze up on.

"We're going to find them."

"Yeah? Then what?"

"We stop them."

# Chapter Eighteen

"Eiri you gotta go see a doctor I'm telling you it's not going to heal properly. We're gonna end up cutting your dam arm off or something for crying out loud."

"Grant we're not having this conversation again I am fine, my arm is fine. Just some cosmetic damage, it doesn't feel like it looks."

"At least wrap it so it doesn't get infected then."

Eiri really wasn't fine but he hadn't told Grant about the Greg altercation, all the old man knew was that he was out here hiding cause one day he got abilities. That was all he needed to know right now. Eiri couldn't risk being recognized and hauled away. It was already almost too much just being back in the city, even if it had been years since they'd left. This was only going to be a temporary reconnaissance mission but the stories they'd been hearing about the powered duo had piqued their interest enough that they had managed to ascertain that they were in fact real and not just fabricated stories so they had to see them for themselves. Eiri's left arm was now definitive proof that the duo was real as real could be and they were not prepared for what they had thrown at them. And by that Eiri meant either side, Eiri knew they had caught them off guard just as much as Eiri and Grant had been surprised by them, it was near poetry and Eiri had to find them.

"What's that plant you put on burns? It's in all the lotions and stuff now."

"Aloe Eiri, you want the Aloe stuff for burns."

"That's it. I'm going to go stop at the store and look for some and maybe some more wraps for it. I'm going to be okay I just got to be smart about this ok old man?"

"Whatever you say Eir."

Grant knew he wouldn't grab anything for it but that wasn't his battle at the end of the day. If the kid wanted to lose an arm who was he to stop him? Even with one arm Eiri was a creature of nature, he was too strong to let this stop him and Grant knew it but he couldn't help but to look after him. Eiri was still a young man, prone to impulse and emotion. Grant understood it, after all he had been there once himself. God how he missed those days sometimes, but Grant had come to learn that looking back never got anyone forward. Perhaps there was a time for such recollection but rarely had Grant afforded himself the time to sit alone with his thoughts; he hadn't allowed himself to since…since the accident. They led nowhere nice and often the panicky feeling that accompanied said thoughts was never a walk in the park to deal with. Grant had grown good at keeping himself busy enough to ward off the feeling. It's how he chose to cope and as unhealthy as it was, according to his oldest sister, he didn't know where to go to sort it out anyway. He was raised to be tough and so tough he was to be, simple as that.

A news bulletin flashed on the screen that caught Grant's eye.

"A downtown fire at a historic building has left the public enraged and investigators stunned."

A voiceover came on with pictures of the building that Eiri and Grant had met the duo.

"Authorities don't know what happened here or who the perpetrators were but camera footage close to the scene show two men walking toward the building prior to the fire….I'm getting something now. This just in now, one of the two men may have been involved in an assault a few years back and is wanted for questioning in connection with that incident."

A blurry picture of Eiri came on the screen and a short story on how he had injured a group of people and left one in critical condition and paralyzed.

"Police are urging the public to not approach the suspect and to call police immediately if a sighting occurs."

When the report ended Grant just sat there stunned staring at the screen.

"I was going to say something ya know?"

Grant didn't realise Eiri had returned and as he turned to face him, Eiri's face looked like it had changed.

"What happened Eir? Did they attack you? Do they know?"

"They did and they don't so don't worry about it. If it interfered with the plan I would have told you and it won't so I didn't."

"Yeah no that's okay I'm just worried. We can't afford to be exposed. Not yet anyway."

"Grant I know. I'm not stupid, this is after all my plan and I'd appreciate if you saw it as such now if you want to question and whine then your usefulness will have run its course. Am I clear?"

"You wouldn't have gotten ten steps into this plan of yours without me do you hear Mr. Plan? Not ten dam steps, hell you didn't even have anything remotely close to a plan until I asked so don't give me that hero crap. I know the plan because you didn't come up with it yourself."

Eiri knew he was right, he had spoken out of turn and Grant wasn't exactly a softie. Eiri had slipped and now his anger was leading him into things. He had to turn it around.

"I know I know I just.….I'm projecting I see that. I made a mistake and now I'm taking it out on you I know I'm just…I'm worried too ya know?"

"We have got to keep our heads with this one. This is the real deal now you saw what that lady did. Damn near launched us into next week and that firestorm outta nowhere? They are exactly who we were looking for. We can't go in guns blazing next time or we'll all kill each other before this is over. We need them Eir or this will never work."

Again Eiri knew Grant was right. He'd lost control when they needed it the most, but if truth were told Eiri had simply gotten scared. And the threat sent him into survival mode, even with a bum arm he had tracked them into the alley and had almost taken them out with a garbage bin until the woman stopped it. That's what got Eiri. All his strength, all his might went into hurling that bin at them and she turned instantly and overpowered Eiri which caused the bin to ricochet back into the alley. And that frightened Eiri even more. In three years he hadn't felt fear as he worked through his abilities and yet this woman stopped him in his tracks. What was he doing wrong? He knew he had some work to do and once he figured it out, he would stop her. Now it was personal.

"Let it go Eiri I know that look. You're planning something else now aren't you? They are not our enemy!"

"Yeah? Friendlies don't shoot first then ask questions after the fact."

"WE shot first Eir!"

"No. We gave them a warning. Now it's war."

"I don't like it Eir aren't we supposed to be recruiting them? Isn't that the mission?"

"It was."

"Dammit Eir we don't have to...."

"We don't really need them and if there is even a small chance that they could stop us we have to remember that and we have to stop them first. No buts."

"Goddamit Eir....ok fine what are we going to do?"

Eiri ran over a few scenarios in his head and he couldn't decide what to go with.

"Wait. What was your plan? Befriend them?"

"Well yeah not so much a plan as an action. They're like us why wouldn't we join with them or have them join us? Survival thing yeah?"

Eiri thought to himself again. Befriend them dismantle from the inside. Keep the loyal and kill the ones who fight the cause.

"You know what? You take point. I'll follow this one."

"Yeah? Ok good. I can get behind that, I think I know how to draw them out a little less aggressively.

"Let's do it Grant. I'm with you on this one."

"K so here's what we do…"

~

"Ev!"

"Hey Ev!"

Evelyn's eyes shot open. Someone was calling her.

"Yeah?"

"You've gotta see this now. Come here!"

Evelyn sat up and looked at her alarm clock. It was already eight in the evening. She'd lain down after their last outing and apparently she needed some rack time. She felt groggy, like she'd slept too long.

"Ev!"

"I'm coming!"

Christ were they pushy this evening. She had literally just opened her eyes for crying out loud. Evelyn got to her feet and half assed it up the stairs. She was still stiff from the encounter and she needed proper treatment. They didn't have that here and she damn sure couldn't risk going to a hospital. Evelyn wasn't sure what she could do if put under anaesthetic, so she just avoided that option for the time being.

"What the hell are you screaming about Shorty? I was asleep ya know?"

Shorty didn't say anything he just pointed forward.

Evelyn looked at the television that Shorty was gesturing to. On the screen was a news report that was displaying a large fire on the wires of the Walterdale Bridge. The flames were in the shape of two large triangles. One had a line going through towards the top of it. What did they mean? Who put it there?

"We did some quick research on the symbolic meaning of the triangles and well we're almost sure it's a message."

"Yeah? To who? What's it say?"

"It's to you Ev. And Will. They're the astrological symbols for Air and Fire."

# Chapter Nineteen

The under belly of the bridge surprised Evelyn, it wasn't like she hadn't been under bridges before but this one was unique. Its walkway didn't suspend directly under it, rather it went off to the side and levelled off with the road it paralleled. So she wasn't entirely sure where to meet whoever had made the signal. A sudden voice broke the silence.

"Hey there."

Ev turned around half expecting to be hit by an attack. Fortunately no such attack came.

"What is this? Who are you?"

"We've actually met, though regrettably that didn't go so well."

"You're the ones who attacked us."

"As I said previously, our first encounter regrettably didn't go over as good as I'd hoped it would."

"How do I know this doesn't go the same? Why shouldn't I toss you into that wall and be done with it?"

"Because I'd crush your bones from the inside if you touched him."

"Eiri dammit not now, you promised."

The second voice retreated back into the shadows. Evelyn knew that whoever that was, was definitely in charge.

"Let me talk to him. He's calling the shots isn't he?"

"You'll speak to me just fine. I'm Grant."

"Well I'm Ev, if that really matters. Why are we here Grant?"

"Because we're just like you and we want to show you."

Evelyn's knees began to shake. After meeting Ben and William she had always wondered whether or not she would ever find anyone like them or if they were all just by chance.

"How do you plan on showing us Grant? Throwing us off this bridge into the water? Cause that seemed to be the answer you went to last time. We weren't even given a chance."

"We're sorry for all that, it was just a misunderstanding and we want to make it up to you. We know a place. It's a small pub just down the road. No powers in public, no attention. That's our only request."

"We hope you'll join us."

After a short back and forth with William, the duo made their way to the pub that Grant had mentioned. It was definitely small and out of the way, Ev had been sure she'd walked by or down this road but she had never noticed this place. Perhaps that was the charm.

Evelyn and Will entered the bar at ten o'clock, they scanned the room and found Grant sitting in a booth towards the back corner. A younger man sat with him, his head down.

"Care for some drinks," Grant asked as the duo approached.

"No thanks, we don't trust you so we're going to stay sober for this."

"Suit yourself. They make a great tequila sunrise. Just saying."

As the two sat down and got comfortable in their seats, the shadowed figure in the back of the booth lifted his head to garner a look at them.

"So what can you two do?"

Evelyn felt shocked to hear someone that wasn't in their hideout ask them what they were capable of without threatening arrest or worse. As off-putting as it felt, she also felt relieved knowing that for once she may be able to answer truthfully. She just had to be careful.

Evelyn looked towards Will and he nodded, then she raised her hand towards Eiri and pulled back.

Eiri knew once the two sat down that was indeed the two that he had attacked in the alley. He had an idea of what she was capable of but he didn't know what her partner could be so while throwing caution to the wind he just straight out asked them.

The girl didn't say anything in return, she only glanced at her partner and stuck her hand out towards Eiri. Then she closed it and pulled back.

At once Eiri felt his breath grow thin. Then he felt it being pulled from his lungs, like deep within him it was being ripped out, he couldn't breathe. He stuck his arm out and threw the girl back in her seat, pinning her against the booth chair.

She lowered her closed fist and let her arm fall to the table. Eiri felt the air return to his body, he took a deep breath and realised what she had just done.

A certain fear filled Eiri as he began to realise just what had happened. He looked up at the girl and for once he felt a weird sense of belonging and for the first time in a long time, Eiri smiled.

"You're the air aren't you, and he's the flame."

"Yeah something like that, so what's that make you two," Will asked.

There was a bit of a silence before Grant stuck his hand out towards Will's cup of water. While he did the liquid inside it began to rise and spiral upwards, as if it were dancing into a water spout. It rose up and up and jumped into the empty cup Evelyn had sitting in front of her.

"I'm the water."

The group looked at once towards Eiri. Of the entire group he was the last to showcase what he could do, but truth be told he wasn't even sure. He couldn't control the elements like the rest of them could and honestly he didn't know the extent of what he could do. But he did know he could mess with the lights and so he would go with that…for now.

Evelyn was impressed with Grant's water trick. It made her wonder how much water he could move or if the weight even mattered. She looked to the other man, waiting to see what he was capable of. The man knew they were looking and after a slight hesitation he put his palm up towards the ceiling and closed it. As he closed his fist the whole place went dark.

The instant intense dark scared Evelyn, she felt uneasy like whatever was happening shouldn't be happening. It made her very nervous.

"That's enough Eir."

On cue the lights came back, the music came back and the humming noise that Ev hadn't noticed before also came back. It was like the whole place got hit by a pause button, it went so silent and so still.

"That was you," Will was caught off guard by what the stranger just did and he felt increasingly curious. He didn't like it, it felt… wrong.

The small group sat in silence for a moment or two.

"Yeah I get that a lot."

Eiri knew he had just frightened the two but that was his intention. Grant had come to possibly recruit the two into what a superhuman group thing but not Eiri. Eiri had come to put the fear of him into them and judging by their current state, he felt he had done just that.

"If you liked that, you're going to love this one."

Eiri pointed at a small mess of empty beer bottles sitting on the bar, A small jolt of electricity shot forth from his extended finger and flew into the bottles, shattering them all in a blue light. The man sitting at the bar next to them fell off his stool in surprise. The group watched in awe and of course this made Eiri laugh. The man who had ended up on the ground noticed the laugh.

"Think that was funny jackass," the man said walking towards the table. He had his eye on Eiri and he didn't look too happy.

"Want to throw another one? Come on tough guy."

The man thought Eiri threw a bottle, which worked in the group's favor. When he got close enough he pulled Grant out of the booth and shoved him aside. He began reaching for Eiri when he was suddenly propelled backwards onto the ground flat on his back. A few patrons who were watching intently helped the man off the ground, that's when Eiri noticed that they all seemed to have the same jacket on. This was going to be a bit of a problem.

Suddenly Eiri was blindsided and tackled by one of them, the surprise take down managed to have Eiri land on his bad arm and for a minute he was vulnerable. The redheaded man who tackled Eiri to the ground was about to lay in some punches when he was suddenly thrown into the bar by Evelyn.

"Get off of him!"

Evelyn barely had time to think after Eiri got taken to the floor, all she knew was that the group of men in the jackets all began to approach him and that was not going to end well.

She threw one of them into the bar and stood in a defensive stance. Will and Grant also stepped in between the group and Eiri, they too were at the ready.

There was the briefest of pauses between the two groups, the bar fell silent as the scene played out.

"Get em," one of the largest men Evelyn had ever seen said to the rest of his friends.

"Move and then get ready to run."

Evelyn heard Eiri but before she could turn to talk to him, he moved her aside and stood up.

Laid out on the ground with pain coursing through him brought back a feeling Eiri had not remembered in a long time. He didn't like the feeling and he could feel the rage coming. His arms began to burn and his vision slightly blurred. Eiri knew what he had to do. He moved the girl aside and stood up to the men. He raised his arms and with all his might he pushed as hard as he could with an outward extension of his rage. All the lights went out as he did.

~

When the lights came back on and Evelyn's hearing began to return all she could hear was the screams. Through the dust and smell of something that she couldn't quite place, what had just happened began to come clear. Torn clothing and blood covered the bar's back wall. Some of the wall had been blown away revealing the alley behind the bar and people were running out however they could. They were slipping and falling and screaming and Evelyn knew whatever just happened shouldn't have. Suddenly Will was grabbing her by the arm and telling her that they had to leave now. There was no sign of the other two. They must have already gotten out.

"Will what just…."

"I know I know well I mean I don't know but we gotta keep moving for now okay Ev?"

"Yeah no let's get the hell out of here."

Evelyn couldn't sleep that night. Her and Will had gotten back and instead of reporting what happened they told their people that it was just a meet and greet and there were others like them out there. She didn't know why they didn't tell them but her and Will came to an understanding and that led to them not telling the others what exactly had transpired.

A sudden phone ringing from her jacket caused Evelyn to nearly jump out of her skin. She hurriedly reached for her pocket and pulled out a cellphone she had never seen before. Unknown Number was calling but Evelyn was sure she knew who it was.

"Who is this?"

"That was a hell of a first meeting wasn't it?"

Evelyn recognized the voice but she never directly got his name.

"The name is Eiri. It's nice to meet you."

# Chapter Twenty

Sometimes Eiri sat and just thought, a lot of those times the thoughts gave him the feel. He called it the Feel because it was something different and he felt it in his bones. Today it was about her and whenever he thought about her he needed a drink. That's just how it worked. He had heard enough to know that he was creating an unhealthy coping technique for feelings that could be worked out but Eiri being Eiri he allowed the Feel to permeate him sometimes. Like that little bit of heart racing anxiety he caused himself showed that he was still in fact alive. Sometimes he felt so numb that maybe this was his drug of choice. To not feel and to dig in and remain comfortable with the only solace he could find, buried in his pain. As the thoughts came to him and he allowed them to, Eiri closed his eyes.

"Where do you think you're going loser?"

Eiri thought he was home free this time but the voice told him he hadn't quite made it out fast enough. Maybe if he just made it out the door they'd leave him alone.

"Hey weirdo I'm talking to you!"

Eiri tried his best to ignore the group but they were persistent, on an almost daily basis they confronted him, he never understood why. He kept to himself mostly and didn't try to bug anyone. What was he doing so wrong?

The largest of the boys, Edward (last name starting with an E), grabbed Eiri by the collar of his coat, spun him around and then threw him to the ground.

"I said where do you think you're going weirdo? You haven't cried yet today and you know that's how this goes."

Eiri knew just that, the boys would kick him now. They would probably pull his hair too, since that's just what they did and Eiri wasn't strong enough to stop them. There was just too many of them.

Once the group of boys let up and Eiri was left shaking on the ground with tears rolling down his face, he'd barely find the strength to stand up. This daily occurrence was taking its toll on Eiri and lately he faked sick so he wouldn't have to come to school and deal with the boys and their bullying. Today was different though.

"Leave him alone you bunch of jerks!"

The voice sounded like an angel.

As Eiri was beginning to stand up a hand came out of nowhere and offered him help. When Eiri saw the hand initially he cowered but a calming voice assured him it was okay. Eiri glanced up to see who the hand belonged to and he lost his strength all over again.

"Hi. My name is Elena, do you need some help?"

Eiri allowed the girl to help him to his feet and he even secretly brushed away his tears so she didn't notice them.

"Thank you," Eiri stuttered through a shaking voice.

"Those guys are losers, don't let them get to you."

Eiri shook his head in agreement. He knew this to be true and he wished he could make them pay for their unnecessary aggressiveness but he didn't have it in him to act on it. Not like how she stood up to them, it made Eiri feel weird inside.

"What's your name? Are you new here? Do those guys do that all the time? Do you want a friend?"

The girl was full of questions but Eiri didn't mind them, it was just nice for him to have someone talk to him that wasn't making fun of him. Or yelling at him for things he didn't understand. He tried to answer them all but she was rattling them off so quickly Eiri couldn't get to them each one.

"I'm Eiri. I've always been here. Yes they do."

"You forgot one."

Eiri didn't want to answer the last one. Did he need a friend? Yes inside he supposed he did but friends never lasted and most ended up making fun of him anyway. Eiri felt afraid to answer it, he didn't want to scare her away too. Eiri looked at her and as he did something in her eyes told him he'd be okay. She wasn't going to scare off anywhere.

"You don't have to answer now ya know? But I will keep bugging you until you answer okay? Also I like your name, it's weird. I like weird. I think I'm weird. Maybe we'll be weird together Eiri."

From that day on Eiri had an actual friend when he went to school and they remained close throughout the years.

One evening Eiri had gone with his adoptive father to a work event. Eiri didn't want to go but reluctantly he did and fortunately he had. It was the usual dinner party setting and shortly after arriving Eiri was walking to go to the bathroom.

"Hi friend."

Upon hearing the voice Eiri froze, he recognized it and so he turned around. There stood Elena and Eiri learned that day that as it turned out their dads worked for the same company. "Hi back friend."

And he called her that because after many days of repeatedly asking Eiri accepted her friend invitation. It scared him but he knew he had to try. So as time went the two and their families became entangled through various get-togethers. Birthday parties, barbecues, swimming pools and water parks were just some of the things their families did together as the two grew up. As cliché as it sounded, the two became inseparable.

Eiri remembered the day he had asked her to graduation. He had been absolutely terrified all day prior to actually asking her the question itself. Though everything was going for him, rather for them, he had it in the back of his mind that she would say no when he asked.

"Where are we going?"

"You'll see Elena; I promise you're going to love it. I found the place while exploring."

The trees broke open into a small clearing that led to a perfect view overlooking the river that flowed through the south part of town.

"My god Eiri it's beautiful!"

Eiri felt his heart flutter.

"Yes it really is. I'm glad you like it. Um so Elena?"

"Yes Eiri?"

"I know that we…uhh I mean you and I are good friends and all but I have a question for you."

"Mhm go on."

"We're graduating soon and well I…."

Elena leaned in and kissed him and it threw Eiri completely off guard. He didn't even have to finish his question.

"I would love to go with you. In every lifetime Eiri and I mean every one, it'll always be us."

A smile lit up his face and Eiri knew he loved her right then.

Eiri was able to be completely himself around her and so he shared things with her he never told anyone else, intimate things that even those workers he had to go see never knew. He didn't really tell them what they needed to hear but he got awful good at saying what they wanted to hear. Eiri had always felt his whole life was bound to be him pretending to be someone else and it made his head hurt sometimes. He often thought he didn't think like everyone else nor worry about the things other people worried about. Even school pushed him on paths that didn't interest him, he always thought there was more to life than what everyone else was doing. He also felt that Elena felt the same way about things and how they work. Perhaps that's why he fancied her so. They were in some ways the same but in other things they saw completely opposite sides of the coin, though one could call that complementing and complemented each other they did.

Eiri's arms began to tingle and it brought him back to reality.

It was 1:33 in the morning.

Eiri reached for the phone to call the girl. It was time.

Evelyn knew he was right, she should have said something but they weren't like her, she feared how they would see her after that. It was selfish but it was for her well-being.

"You're right and I'm sorry about all that it just took some sorting out in my own head you know? It's been stuck with me since and I can't figure it out."

"Figure what out Ev," Karyn asked. The look on her face seemed like she genuinely wanted to help.

"How do we stop him?"

The words cut the tension in the room and as Evelyn said it, the front door blew across the room and went through the far window.

~

"After the accident Grant how many of those people actually helped you? Or was it just sign here date here and here's your money?"

"I'm sure they tried Eir but I wasn't in any place to even want to accept their help so…."

Eiri cut him off before he finished. Eiri had a plan and that meant he had to push.

"What about the farmer? Did he get any kind of punishment?"

"Well no but…"

"Shouldn't he have?"

"Well yeah I mean he probably…"

"Then let's give it to him."

"What do you mean Eiri?"

"We're going for a drive Grant. There's something we got to do."

Grant knew better than to argue with him, Eiri had been keeping them functional and Grant began to trust him. Maybe his methods were unorthodox but they got results and that's what they kept doing. Grant was his muscle when needed and Eiri led them to opportunities and jobs that Grant wouldn't have been able to find. How Eiri did it he didn't know so a level of trust was necessary. Eiri was reckless sometimes and jumped to conclusions and he never asked before doing anything but he was young and with a different mind than Grant. His was the mind they needed and so Grant followed him.

"Okay Eiri."

Grant hopped in the car after grabbing his water bottle. Even now Grant wanted a drink and holding something in his hand helped kill the urge a little. Eiri drove so Grant was able to relax in the passenger seat, as he relaxed he thought of trust and slowly he closed his eyes.

A couple hours later Grant opened his eyes and the car was stopped. The air felt cooler.

When his eyes adjusted to the light and he could see again, he saw it. That damn bridge. Eiri had brought them to the accident site.

Grant stepped out of the car and for the first time in a long time he gazed upon the spot that had taken the last little bit of light out of him. His arms began to tingle.

"You feel that? That small bit of rage building up? That's what I feel Grant, all the time and so I understand your pain."

"Why are we…"

"Because I needed you to feel it and you had to remember it."

Grant's shoulders began to tingle now. It was building.

"We can use that pain Grant. We can make them see, we can make them all see. We can force them to see their choices, how they treat people that aren't on their paths or doing their work. This whole world is going to shit and we got a chance here to do something about it because of what we can do. These so called leaders that tell us what to do and how to do it and then themselves do it differently, they don't make sense anymore. They try to be respected and approved so everyone likes them and that's not working. We're the next step Grant and we can do something I know it. You just have to take the leap."

Grant listened to Eiri's words and as he did he felt the tingling subside, like it comforted him to hear the words from someone else. Grant couldn't lie, he too lost faith in the world after Elizabeth and Ben were taken from him. Eiri was right when he spoke of how people treated him after it all. Grant tried to speak of truth about the accident but no one listened or believed him. Grant destroyed the bridge with his bare hands was not something the courts or cops wanted to even listen to. They didn't care, Grant often felt like just an afterthought to them when he actually tried to get help. As he remembered everything he felt during and after the accident, the water closest to Grant began to churn and move.

Grant had at least attempted to go get some help after Ben passed and he came up empty handed. Each door that attempt led to ended up being a bureaucracy of nonsense and costly so at the end of the day, Grant gave up.

Eiri's honeyed words and the setting for Grant's pain tipped the scales in his mind. He'd do whatever Eiri wanted done. And that was leading him right now to the old farmer not far upstream.

"Let's go see Mick."

"That is a splendid idea Grant."

~

"Hey kid make sure you spread the grain all away along the trough ok? They're smart but sometimes two will try to fit into one spot."

"Yes sir, I can definitely do that."

Mick still liked the kid, which was rare given how the revolving door of farm hands that went through the place. Most just couldn't cut it and Mick often told them so.

While the kid fed the heifers, Mick took in the view off to his right across the creek. The trickling water often calmed the old man down when the days got too hot. Today it relaxed him as the last bit of ice from the winter melted away, it had been a long winter and Mick was glad it was finally over.

"Hey sir I think we're going to fetch a little more…."

Bryan was cut off as a large barrage of water and ice hit him square in the chest and sent him flying backwards into some straw.

Mick could barely react to what had just happened when suddenly he was suspended in the air, as if an invisible force was picking him up by his collar.

"Look what we have here Grant, the old man who got away with it."

Mick didn't recognise the man from where the voice came, it confused him even more.

"Mick."

Mick knew that voice from the many times he heard it in the courtroom. It was the man who lost his boy. The man whose face he saw often in his dreams or more accurately his nightmares. Mick knew what was coming.

"Mr. Thomas I'm sorry…"

The first bit of ice hit him hard enough it pierced his shoulder. Mick winced and gasped, unable to really move. The pain burned and traveled down his arm. The next shot hit him in both legs, Mick was sure his left one broke under the immense pressure that the force came at him with.

"God please stop."

"Grant wait, I want him to see this."

The water stopped hitting him in the face and Mick was turned around in the air so he could see the pens of his cattle. This corner of the farm had his heifers, all his beautiful girls.

Suddenly the ground began to rise under the fencing surrounding the pens. A loud metallic groaning filled the air and all at once the fences lifted high up in the air, slammed together and then dropped. Mick tried to yell, he tried to kick out of whatever held him. That's when the water began to hit him in the face again. Whoever it was had dropped all that iron, onto all his beautiful girls.

"Stop, please stop."

Mick wasn't even sure his voice was getting past the constant stream hitting him in the face. He tried his darned best though because at this rate knew he would eventually drown. Someone would hear him, they would have to. He had other farmhands, where were they?

What a way to go Mick thought. What a way to go. Perhaps it was some weird form of justice from the universe.

Then the darkness took him.

~

The ride home from the attack site didn't involve much for words. Grant was lost in thought, his conscience for whatever reason wasn't actually doing what he thought it would be doing, it was rather quiet. This made Grant even more apprehensive. When Grant looked to Eiri he noted that he looked rather calm rather than anxious. This should have made Grant nervous but instead it made him feel relaxed. Trusting.

When they arrived back to the city, Eiri stopped to grab a bottle of whisky and Grant followed suit by picking up some vodka. This was going to be one of those nights and Grant was totally okay with it leading them into the early morning. Today was a lot and he needed some help to process what exactly they had done.

"So Grant today was just the beginning steps of a winding staircase that will lead us to where we want to be ok? I know it was a lot but we…."

"Eiri I am on board. People need to see."

Grant didn't need him to finish his sentence, he was in. To hell with people this society needed a reset anyway. Maybe that was Grant's real purpose, to help usher in this new….whatever this was.

"Also hey I found out where that pair of interesting individuals we met at the bar stay."

"Are we going to pay them a visit?"

"I think we should."

"Alright Eir."

When Grant slept he dreamed, he dreamed of dark things.

# Chapter Twenty-Two

The sound of their front door hitting their back wall caused the whole team to simultaneously duck. Startled yells and cries of confusion filled the room and luckily for the team no one had been on the other side of that door.

"Anybody home?"

Evelyn knew the voice, it was Eiri. He'd found them.

They at least had home field advantage for whatever was going down and Evelyn had an idea on how to use that.

She ducked and darted down the hall for the first room on the left. That was her room for whatever she wanted to use it for, it normally was where she slept though at first that wasn't what its intended use was going to be. It was going to be an office of sorts, a work place kind of deal. She even had Candy's urn in there. It was the last special place for her.

A loud splintering noise echoed through the building as she turned into her doorway. Evelyn wondered what it was. Hopefully everyone was okay out there. She wasn't sure how to stop Eiri but at least she did have an idea on how to slow him down.

The way the place was built ended up so that Ev's room was almost adjacent to the front entrance; the door opening bothered her all night most nights. Evelyn figured that if that's where they were standing well perhaps maybe she could surprise them.

Evelyn got her hands raised up and was about to push the wall into the entrance when it suddenly flew towards her instead.

Some of the wall broke as it hit her; most of it stayed together and allowed for her to be pinned under it as it crossed the threshold into her bedroom.

"Nice try. I'd have tried the same thing."

"Eiri what are you doing?"

"Tipping the scales."

Evelyn couldn't see what was happening but she could hear the screams from her team as Eiri went through the apartment. Wood splintering and loud crashing noises filled the air. She had to get out there.

Okay Evelyn snap out of it. Your arms are pinned yes but maybe if you could just shift a little and push outward, maybe that'll do it. Evelyn was finding it harder to breathe, her arms felt like jelly as she tried to at least move one of them. She squirmed and shimmied and once a little bit of movement from her hand became available she would be able to, yes she got one out…..the wall pinning her went flying back across the room towards their front door. She was free.

The sound of water rushing made it hard to hear what was happening around her, she would have to be careful. Eiri turned the tables and before her team even began to deal with him, he had taken the element of surprise and used it against them. How did he find them she wondered to herself?

There was smoke and water running everywhere, some dust filled the room so the place looked like a warzone, but yet she heard no movement from people. Where was everyone? Had she been pinned longer than she thought? Was she too late? Were they all…a shuffling noise had her crouching for cover.

"Eiri?"

"Ev?"

It was Will's voice that answered. Thank god.

"Will where are you? Is he still here?"

"No, I don't think so. I think they took Ben."

"Shh. Just wait. Yup I hear voices. This has to be it."

"Okay Eiri so what is the…."

Grant wasn't able to complete his thought when Eiri blew the door off the hinges into the hideout. This was going to be interesting. Grant wasn't even sure what they were doing here and so he decided to give Eiri a little space to work out whatever he was dealing with on why he wanted to come here to see them. So Grant watched.

"Anybody home?"

Grant thought Eiri to act like a cat when it came to these types of missions or whatever they would do when they needed supplies or money. Eiri stalked and played with the people they'd intimidate, much like a bobcat would do while hunting. Grant also knew once Eiri tired of play, he was ruthless.

Now that they had gotten their attention Eiri raised his hand up and pulled a pipe out of the wall and then he split it apart at one of its seams. The burst pipe sprung forth large amounts of water everywhere. This caused Eiri to turn to Grant.

"Your turn, I got the girl."

Eiri stepped back into the entranceway and placed his palm on one of the walls. Then he pushed and the wall flew apart inside the building.

Grant turned his attention to the burst pipe. He focused on the water pooling on the ground below the broken pipe, he pictured lifting it into one mass of water; it swirled and floated in front of him. From the corner of his eye he caught what he thought to be a flame. So he shot all the water in that direction. The yells that came from that room meant he had hit his mark.

A lady and a man charged at Grant from one of the rooms off to his right, he turned to face them and was almost too late. He still had water pouring out of the burst pipe so he shot it at them and as he did, to his surprise Eiri hit that stream of water with some electricity. The room blacked out for a second and then it turned eerily quiet.

Unbeknownst to the duo attacking, Ben was still hiding in the kitchen. He also had a pistol for this very reason. Once he saw Eiri attack Shorty and Erin he knew he had to take a shot.

~

The man was careful as he crouched but Eiri knew he was watching, maybe waiting for a window. Eiri debated on letting the man try, just to see what would happen but then he decided against that and reached out to the man to grab him. When Eiri felt the cold iron on the man's person he used his full force. He pulled the man across the room and pinned his arms out so the gun fell. Eiri slammed the man upwards into the roof and knocked the man out cold and then he forcefully threw him back down into the floor with such tremendous force that the impact kicked up dust.
"Eiri we gotta go."
"Oh I agree and we're taking this one, I feel something in him. He's not like these other ones. He's strong."

~

Evelyn Towne used to want to peacefully exist in her little corner of the world with her dog and her books. A cup of tea and some rain pattering on the roof of her small awning. Now she was here, burying some of her close friends because she disagreed with someone. This was the world they lived in. She'd read books of heroes and bad guys but this was not so black and white, this was nothing like story books. It was messy and it hurt and it didn't make sense all the time, things used to make sense Ev thought, at least she thought they did. Now she wasn't sure what to think anymore. People kept dying around her. And she remembered them all by name and how they treated her. Such beautiful people and her beloved Candy, my how she missed that dog right now.

So as Evelyn sat through another funeral, she held hope that Ben was still out there; alive and well and waiting for rescue. She'd been trying for a few days and thinking on how they would find them. She didn't know how Eiri did it and so that lead to her feeling inadequate, like she was failing what she started. If she couldn't do this why do any of it at all? This was crunch time and she had no idea where to turn. Evelyn Towne was a failure.

"Hey who is that?"

Evelyn heard Will with his question but her mind didn't really care at the moment.

"I've seen them before, but not here. Hey Ev you listening?"

Ev was not.

"Well I'm going to talk to them."

Evelyn watched Will approach the figure. She watched as the stranger handed Will something and then she watched the stranger promptly leave. What was it? Evelyn finally let her mind stray from Eiri and walked over to Will.

"Who was that? What'd they give you?"

"Hope."

Evelyn looked at the paper. It was a phone number and one word. Chen.

# Chapter Twenty-Three

"Where am I?"

"Eiri he's awake."

"Ahh I was beginning to lose faith in your resilience, I wouldn't have been surprised if you'd been out all night. I told you Grant, he's strong."

"You're the guy from the bar. What is this?"

"This, my friend, is what you would call a turning point I would suppose."

"What the hell does that mean?"

"Yours to be exact and you don't have to rush it, you have to choose."

"Eiri maybe we should talk to him. Wouldn't that be ea…"

"He's got this Grant why don't we just give him a minute."

The two then left the man alone to go hash out a plan, because abducting someone was not the plan or in the plan at all and Grant needed some clarity.

The pair walked through their place of operations in an awkward silence. Grant never wanted to take one of them or do what they had done at the other group's lair. Did they go too far? Was this the inevitability of the path they were choosing? Perhaps it was too late now. Maybe this was their destiny. Eiri certainly thought so and perhaps that was wearing off on Grant because even if there was conflict on what was happening in Grant's head, he had no plan on changing course. Grant just felt different was all.

"You gotta just let it go. The fight inside will exhaust you if you do not choose."

"What are we going to do with him Eir?"

"I'm not sure yet."

Eiri had made the choice to bring along the man out of impulse. To make the others pay for what they did to his arm. He honestly didn't know what to do with their prisoner but they'd have to figure out who he was and why he was on their side, maybe he was skilled with firearms or something. Their team was relatively small so he had to be important somehow.

---

Ben's whole body hurt. The guy from the bar was stronger than their team's intel had let on and he nearly tore Ben apart.

Where was he?

Was he surrounded by…by dirt? They must be underground.

A stinging pain shot through Ben's arm and up through his shoulder. It caused his vision to blur and he doubled over in duress. Maybe if he just closed his eyes it would subside, maybe just a little rest Ben thought to himself but then the darkness overtook him. Ben slept for hours and when he woke up it was already a new day.

---

"I don't know Grant. We'll let him go eventually; maybe we can just get some information on the girl. I don't know why I did it, I told you it just happened."

"Yeah well you're lucky he woke up again. Do you realise that right now all of those people you just pissed off are looking for us? You realise that right?'

"Yeah and they will never find us."

"Look Eiri I get it, this whole mess got away on us and maybe there's no way out but we gotta let this guy go. He wasn't in the plan, like at all."

A loud noise off towards their captive made the two men jump straight out of their chairs.

"What the hell was that?"

"I don't know Grant I don't see through walls."

Dust filled the hallways as they approached their makeshift prison. As they got closer they saw a hole in the wall and their prisoner had fled through it.

Before Grant could turn to tell Eiri to go easy, Eiri had raced through the hole after the escaping man.

~

Where the hell was he? Nothing but trees surrounded Ben and he had no idea way of knowing which way was which. All Ben knew was that he had to keep moving because whoever had captured him sure wouldn't hesitate to do it again and they were definitely chasing him, he could hear them and every now and then a loud crashing noise could be heard behind him, like they were chopping down trees or something. He turned around quickly and threw up a wall of dirt and grass, hoping to slow them down behind him. Suddenly Ben ran upon a clearing and as he was crossing it he felt his legs stop working. The muscles wanted to keep going but he couldn't move them and suddenly he was lifted up into the air.

~

Eiri was almost upon him, he could see the man now. Tossing trees out of the way definitely helped Eiri know that man wasn't hiding anywhere. He was smart to try and outrun him, distance between them was definitely his best chance of getting away but even now Eiri knew he was gaining. A bunch of ground flew up in front of Eiri, like a wall to stop him. Eiri grinned, so this was the man's power. He was one of them after all, interesting Eiri thought. With one hand raised Eiri blew through the wall of ground and kept on after the man. He could feel the metal on the man's belt buckle and if he concentrated even more then he could feel the man's bones under his skin. Eiri stopped and reached his hand out. The running man instantly froze. Eiri had him now. Eiri lifted his hand up and the man was then suspended into the air a few feet. As he closed the gap between them, Eiri began to turn the man around so that he would be facing him rather than facing the woods in front of them. The man yelled as Eiri slowly began spreading out his fingers.

~

Ben didn't really know what the whole purpose was behind a meaningful life. Maybe it was work hard and retire like everyone did, maybe it was to see the world and appreciate the beauty in it or maybe it was to simply love. These are the thoughts that began to race through his mind as he was being spun in the air to face his captor. He tried reaching out to the earth to stop his attacker but nothing happened, he was unable to move the ground. The pulling Ben felt within his body as the man began to open his hand was more than Ben could take, his muscles felt like they were on fire, his limbs began to feel pressure like he'd never experienced and the pain was excruciating. Ben yelled out as he felt his shoulders and hips popping. The man was tearing him apart. Ben closed his eyes. Then the darkness overtook him.

~

Eiri didn't know any other resolution to the current predicament he had put them in so the attempted escape was the perfect excuse to clean up that particular mess. After stretching the man's body out and almost tearing off his limbs Eiri closed his fist which then caused the man to compact down into a ball of flesh and blood and then Eiri launched this mass into the middle of the lake that was just to the left of the clearing he stood in now. It was done. Problem dealt with Eiri thought to himself and no mess to clean up, even better. Rustling footsteps behind Eiri meant Grant had finally caught up. Guess he missed the show.

"Where is he? Did he get away?"

"Yeah I lost him Grant, sneaky bastard must have doubled back on me or something. He was fast, too fast for me."

"Goddamit Eiri. You know he's going to bring them right back here to us right?"

"Well perhaps we go to them first then. Get ready Grant. We're going hunting."

# Chapter Twenty-Four

The alley they were told to meet the mysterious Chen person looked like the typical back alley meeting place Evelyn had seen in movies. It was always a damn alley. This is where their desperation had taken them; this is what Eiri had driven them to. Meeting strangers in allies, this is how far he'd beat them. Maybe they were about to be abducted and sold into the black market, kidneys and all in a bath tub full of ice and….

"Evelyn they're here, snap out of it."

As Ev looked up, a pair of men in black suits beckoned them to come closer. There was a door behind the men that they motioned for them to enter; nodding like everything was going to be okay.

Will grabbed Evelyn's hand and led her towards the door. The action made Evelyn feel weird but in a comforted kind of way, a way she had not felt in a long time. Maybe everything would be okay after all she thought to herself… just maybe.

After entering the building they were led through a series of rooms that used beaded curtains or the like as doors instead of actual doors. Again like the movies, Evelyn couldn't help but notice.

When they hit the end of this maze of rooms they were met by an older lady sitting on a rickety chair under a beam of sunlight, people working all around her.

"Sit," the lady suggested as they drew closer to her, "we have some things to discuss."

So the pair took up her offer and sat in the chairs opposite her.
"Chen," William asked quietly.
"That is my name yes."

Will wasn't wholly comfortable with what was going on around them, this was clearly some of organization and not just your average run of the mill street gang or what have you. From the minute they entered the building Will had been scanning and keeping his head on a swivel, he wasn't sure how relaxed they could get here.

"Okay Chen I don't mean to be overly forward but we have had a bit of a rough go and I just wanna know who the hell you are and why we're here, okay?"

Chen's response to Will's statement was to simply smile and look at both of them with bright eyes.

"My stars I never thought I'd live to see the day. I can feel you both you know? You must be air, you're almost cold. And you are definitely fire I can tell you got that warmth around you."

Will didn't know what to say or how to answer. The old lady was right but how? Who was she that she knew that much about them while they themselves knew squat. It gave Will the chills.

"Don't fret my friends I mean no harm. Let me show you."

Chen said something to one of her guards and he quickly brought her a jug of water and placed it on the table dead center.

Chen barely moved her hand and all the water lifted up out of the jug and suspended in the air above the table.

"Holy man you're one of us, Evelyn she's one of us!"

"Actually we're one of her or rather…wait. You know what I mean."

"It's been a long time coming and my I've been so alone. I knew more would come though, I never gave up that hope."

"Miss you've gotta do one better, we're not sure we follow here. There was more? What happened to them… also my name is Evelyn."

The water in the jug fell perfectly back into the jug.

"Chen Hong. Water elemental and yes there was more. Three more to be exact but they're not around anymore and haven't been for a long time. The boys in black saw to that."

"What do you mean the boys in black?"

"Exactly what you think of when you think boys in black, the suits, the feds, whatever you prefer."

"What'd they do to the others and why are you still here?"

Ev studied the lady's movements and how she spoke. There was true pain buried there, the lady wasn't lying.

"They gathered us together. Said they needed our help. Once we were all together, they bombed the hell out of the place."

"How'd you survive?"

"I didn't go."

Ev wasn't sure what to think, it was hard to believe something like that could happen. Was that their fate too? The implications behind that mixed with what she believed caused her head to spin.

"Don't worry dear I know what's going to come to pass. You mustn't fret."

"How do you know what's going to happen?"

"A looooot of reading of old texts and what not, believe me, it was a lot. There have been ancient references of more elementals popping up throughout history; you just have to look closely at what's been written. For the most part, it ends up the same. We die….tragically."

~

Will felt it as soon as the old lady said it, they were all to die tragically. So what was the point behind it all if they just ended up six feet under anyways? He felt the flicker he got sometimes, deep in his chest, like an old candle that was too stubborn to go out on its' own, he felt hope. He knew that she had gotten them together for a reason and despite what she was talking about he knew, somehow, that she felt they could change it. William believed in synchronicities and the like, that meant whatever was happening was happening for a reason and they were just scratching the surface of this particular gambit.

"You don't believe that do you?"

Chen sat back, like she was surprised by Will's question.

"Well William not everything should be so set in stone. So yes I believe you could achieve a different outcome, but tell me, where are the rest of you?"

"This is it, this is us. One has already fallen to Eiri's side and we have one missing. They took him, to wherever they hang their hat."

"Well that's not ideal but perhaps still doable. Do you have any idea where they stay?"

"We don't know but we're actively searching for it."

"Well then you better search faster."

# Chapter Twenty-Five

Eiri felt the city's concrete and steel as he walked down its' streets. He chose the street where Greg had jumped him with his goons because it felt almost nostalgic to him after what had occurred. Grant stood by him, a testament to Eiri's vision, which was true loyalty.

"For every building I tear down, I'll reveal its water in the pipes. Use that."

"This is it isn't it Eiri?"

"Yes it is. Let's show them true power."

Eiri looked to the small shop to his right; it looked like they served coffee and some vegan ice cream or something of the sort, whatever latest fad people had fallen in love with and posted on their pages of fake pictures, hiding their true feelings in bad food and tasteless colorful drinks. He gestured his hand outright towards it, with a sweeping gesture he ripped the roof clear off it and sent it tumbling down the street. People screamed and ran out of the building in droves. Eiri could practically feel their fear in the air. He loved it, it invigorated him. He couldn't get enough of the intoxication of it all.

~

Nadia Nicholson sat in her usual café and ordered her usual drink, as she did each evening. Another day of no leads and no real evidence suggesting their elemental friends were still out there. It'd been months since any kind of hit at any level of observance from her and her team. Maybe they were all gone now; maybe they'd given up on whatever mission they'd been on. So here she was, entering old information on her current laptop, like it mattered. God she needed a cigarette, too bad she was six months without one.

A crunching sound suddenly filled the building and it came from above her, a quick look up showed her that the roof was coming off, like a lid on a Tupperware container. Nadia scrambled for her phone.

~

Within twenty minutes of being on Whyte Ave, Eiri had managed to tear down ten buildings and all their business. The power he felt behind reducing a thriving shop to mere rubble made him feel something he couldn't quite place. It was enticing, almost like a drug. Eiri was over the edge now with no turning back so he basked in it, like good cologne.

Some patrol cars rolled up on him at one point but Eiri used the power built up in him to hit them with an electrical force powerful enough to blow them up. The electricity protruded out of his fingertips, it was enticing for him. The power pulled him in, he had to continue and he was far from finished. Eiri turned his gaze to downtown, to the sky scrapers across the valley. That's where the world would witness him, a true testament to raw power. He'd use the bridge that connected the Ave to downtown. That was the plan, even if it meant destroying everything in his path and he meant everything. A passing bus was given no quarter as Eiri lifted it off the ground and launched it into a pizza place across the street. The shrieks and yells drove Eiri to continue, to feel the control he currently felt did something to him and he couldn't stop. As Eiri walked to the bridge he saw a diner that was overlooking the river valley, so people could have a view while they attended to their presumptuous picky palettes. He'd see to it that whoever was getting that particular experience tonight would never forget it, if they made it out. When Eiri got close enough he used all the strength he could muster and he picked the whole diner up, tearing it from its' very foundations. Once he got it high enough off the ground over the trees he threw it down the hill, into the river valley, chefs and all.

~

Grant caught up to Eiri while Eiri was throwing a small diner into the river valley. The amount of power or whatever you want to call it that it took to do what he had just witnessed was enough to make Grant fear Eiri all over again. Yes there was definitely some respect for the young man given all Eiri did for Grant these last few years but sometimes when he glimpsed what Eiri could do, like truly do, it reminded him why he followed him. Eiri was a modern day God like Zeus or Thor of old but in the here and now and instead of being revered as he should be, anyone that would see the actuality of who Eiri was and what he was capable of instead was made afraid. Grant knew better. Eiri was something this world needed, he was the cleanse it so desperately wanted. What seemed like ages ago Grant made it clear in his head to help do whatever he could do to help Eiri with the plan and right now it meant tear everything down and so Grant did his part. Who was he to question a modern day God?

~

Eiri felt kind of nervous as he approached the bridge, it grew every second he got closer to it. Could he actually lift this thing he asked himself in his head, he already doubted himself. Eiri knew he couldn't entertain that thought process or he would surely fail, he picked that one up from the good ol' doc, and so he had to around his mind and he had to believe in the plan. The walk down the hill caught up to Eiri and he realised how much more he should have pushed himself to prepare for all this. For all the work he put into his workout routine he felt rather winded at the moment.

"We're doing it Eir."

"I told you my friend, they wouldn't fight back much and when they tried, they'd fall just as easy."

The police had given them a bit of a wide berth now seeing as whatever they threw at them to deter the onslaught of Eiri's plan was not working. Eiri was too strong now; he'd waited until he was. He'd trained long and hard for this, took shit all his life that put his mind in a place where this was all okay to him, he believed to his core that this was all needed and that made him dangerous. Very dangerous.

When the duo finally got to the bridge there was no traffic on it, police had seen to that once it was obvious where they were headed. That could actually help Eiri right now, after all this was not going to be an easy feat in any sense.

Without any sign of warning a group wearing full tactical gear came out of the trees to the west and tried to surprise Eiri and Grant. A few bullets almost made their mark but Eiri was quicker, he grabbed Grant and dove behind a concrete bench. Without looking Eiri then ripped a bunch of trees out of the ground and as the kill team came for them through the small field, Eiri wiped them off the map with the torn out trees and with enough force that most of the team flew into the river. He then grabbed a helicopter out of the air and dropped it onto whoever survived the tree attack out of the tactical group; no one survived that second offensive maneuver.

Eiri and Grant finally got to their bridge.

"Okay Grant I'm going to pick this thing up and we are going to ride it to downtown. How's that sound?"

"Batshit Eiri, it sounds batshit but I guess that's kind of who we are now."

Eiri felt the steel again, the pavement too. He felt how much weight this thing carried, the supports that dug into the river side on either side. The wires, the cables and the amount they held together. This was going to take a lot. She was never meant to be moved and Eiri was going to be the one that changed the very nature of this structure and for that he would never be forgotten.

"Ok so we're above the river, if they try anything you will be the one to stop them, I'm going to have to stay pretty focused here."

"I got it Eiri. Let's do this."

Eiri thought back and allowed himself to think the thought so he could feel the feel, the rage that built up caused his arms to tingle and he used that to reach deep. He pulled the supports inwards and like legs on a spider they curled in and the bridge began to drop.

They didn't fall very much when Eiri felt an abrupt stop in their descent.

"I got us man!"

Eiri looked to Grant and realised water coming up over both sides of the bridge.

"What?"

Suddenly the bridge began to rise up and Eiri used that momentum to propel it upward and with Grant using the river in tandem, they flew up at a pretty fast pace.

"Quick thinking Grant, you may have just saved our asses!"

Eiri felt the pavement again, he used it like a surfboard or least akin to what he thought you'd do to control a surfboard. He only had to make it a kilometre and a half to reach where he wanted to put it down and that was right in the heart of downtown.

When they got to the avenue that Eiri intended to drop the bridge, Eiri turned them west so they could go down a little further. The bridge bounced off buildings and tore them apart at the same time, her weight was tremendous and she did not fly easily.

When Eiri could finally see the old hotel he knew this was the spot and he wanted to make an impact.

"Hold onto something Grant, we're going down with a little speed."

The bridge landed on Jasper Ave with enough force that dust flew up into the air and darkened the sky for a few minutes. The impact also caused windows to explode and spew broken glass all over the Jasper Ave.

Will's phone rang and jolted him out of a spontaneous nap, he hadn't meant to fall asleep he just planned on laying down on the couch and watching a little TV before heading out to meet Evelyn. His caller ID let him know that she was the one on the other end of this particular phone call.

"Will get ready I'm coming to pick you up. We have to get on this."

"Get on what?"

"Check the news and then get ready, I'm on my way."

Will wasn't sure what to expect when he turned on the local news station but what he saw definitely surprised him to say the least.

*Two unknown assailants attacking downtown Edmonton wreaking havoc and causing extensive property damage. Police are advising everybody to avoid the area and to evacuate if you're in the area.*

Will easily recognized who it was by what they were doing, it was the two that attacked the hideout and took Ben. He'd been waiting for this, he was already ready. First he'd kick their ass then he'd ask where they took Benjamin. By the time Ev arrived to pick him up, Will was pissed.

Eiri wasn't sure how he was supposed to feel after undertaking what he was doing but he couldn't help but smile through his hubris. He was on the path he destined to be on and that felt good internally. That helped drive him to continue his path of destruction towards the city centre.

Eiri saw a small square off to his right; he figured he'd drop the nearest building onto it, to reciprocate how he felt tearing down the idea of what this city stood for. As he reached out to pull down the near structure a piece of wood flew by his face, nearly piercing him.

"Hey tough guy why don't you try pulling that crap on me?"

Eiri glanced over and recognized the woman speaking to him as the lady from the hideout.

"You don't frighten me. Come say…."

A flame hit Eiri in the face and he wasn't able to finish his sentence.

"Feel that asshole? That's what's coming for you."

Eiri instantly knew who was here. The two heroes that planned on stopping them, Eiri knew they couldn't. As much as they would try, they were no match for him; Eiri just had to remind of that.

"Grant!"

~

Grant could feel the water flowing through the lines, it surrounded him. Eiri was ahead of him doing his thing, and so Grant was here doing his, using the torn up water lines to assert his own type of damage.

"Grant!"

Grant heard the voice cutting through the wreckage around him, Eiri needed his help and he needed it right now.

As Grant got closer to Eiri he could see the others through the smoke and dust, he knew at once that they were here to stop them or at least try to.

"The heroes are here Grant, they want us to stop."

"If you don't stop we will tear you apart won't we Ev?"

"You'll try and you'll fail, Grant and I are far too powerful. Try us."

# Chapter Twenty-Six

Evelyn wasn't sure how they were planning on taking these guys down, as she looked around and witnessed the destruction they were causing, the heinous ignorance to the fact that people were dying around them, it frightened her as to what lines they may would need to cross to stop them. Was she capable of such an act? She didn't know and a part of her didn't want to find out. Ev had to ask him.

"What is this? Why are you doing this?"

"Do seals ask the shark why it feeds upon them, no because that's just the natural order of things. That's why the apex exists, to quell the lesser."

"So that's all we are to you? The lesser?"

Evelyn once thought she could reason with the man, but after listening to him now, she understood what she had to do and that it wouldn't be easy.

"Is that what Benjamin was to you? A lesser person so you took him? Did you kill him?"

Evelyn's eyes scanned for what lay around her, for an opportunity to strike, quick enough that maybe he wouldn't notice until it was too late. Then she saw it, a sign uprooted from the concrete. She had to move fast.

Grant felt a falter in how he felt about this once he realised that the man they had taken was named Benjamin, like his dear Benny. The man hadn't gotten back to the group, so where was he Grant wondered. Did Eiri actually lose him in those woods by the lake or had Eiri been lying to him?

"You all sit here and act like this city, this world is a pretty place and never once think about the rest of us. The underdogs, the downtrodden the ones who fantasize what it would be like to live a life of normalcy, free of pain and strife and when it comes time to hear us not one of you believe us. Can you even fathom what that does to a person? I bet you can't because you don't have to worry about things like that and yet you complain on and on that life is hard and you have no idea the meaning of such a statement. Hide away in your false pain and act like you got it bad, you don't know pain but you will, you all will because I'm going to show you and when you finally realise the depths of how bad you messed this all up, it'll be too late and you will all have witnessed the mistake of pissing off the wrong person."

Evelyn reached out for her temporary battle axe and as she did Eiri struck outward as well, he sent her flying backwards about half a block. Well he wasn't lying about being formidable, he just proved that his reflexes had definitely been honed to that of a tactical standard.

Grant couldn't seem to shake the whole Benjamin thing, he had to know and so he would ask Eiri.

"The man's name was Benjamin?"

"What Grant? I don't know, I never knew. Why does that matter?"

"Did you kill him Eiri?"

"Grant I…yes I did I'm sorry I misled you I just didn't mean for…"

"Eiri….my son. His name was Benjamin."

Grant's past came rolling over him like a train, it caused him to shake and it began to ground Grant, like he had been on autopilot for the last few years. Grant felt different.

"Maybe this was a sign. Eiri I have to…"

"Don't you dare lose your way on me now Grant because we are so close to finishing this thing."

"You lied to me Eiri and you killed Benjamin."

Grant felt his arms begin to burn, his muscles began to shake. He looked up at Eiri and he felt his eyes change, a deep rage overcame them.

"Grant what are you doing?"

"I need to just go for a walk Eir. I'm struggling here."

Grant needed to put some space between himself and Eiri, he had a plan.

As Grant began to walk away he realised he was standing in a puddle. The water had come from a busted fire hydrant that was releasing a bunch of water onto the street. This was his chance. Maybe it was some form of redemption but he'd buried how he felt about losing Liz and their beautiful son. Instead of dealing with it he chose to ignore it and with doing so it festered inside like a bad sliver. He hadn't even spoken his late son's name in years so the shock of hearing it shook Grant to his core and it broke his resolve. What had he done? Why did he stand with this? How many sons did he allow to die today? How many lives had just joined Eiri in destroying? It had to stop.

Grant got a little closer to the broken fire hydrant and then he spun around, as he did he grabbed a large body of water then he propelled it as hard as he could towards the unsuspecting Eiri.

Suddenly Grant's world went black.

He couldn't tell how much time had passed but when Grant opened his eyes he realised there were two figures standing over him, their hands outstretched, offering help up.

Grant smiled and took their hands.

"We've been waiting for you."

"I'm sorry it took so long, I just got stuck."
"It's okay. Welcome home honey."

~

A large flame down the street indicated that Will had attacked the duo now as well and Evelyn had to get back into the fray because Will couldn't take them alone.

Come on Ev get up and shake off the cobwebs, god her shoulder hurt, she'd have to ignore that for now, there were people counting on her.

As she got to her feet she saw through the dust that the flame down the road grew brighter and more intense and then suddenly it went out.

Oh no they got Will, Evelyn thought, she'd already failed.

The body of Will flying down the street and bowling into Evelyn knocked her back into the pavement once again. Evelyn knew what she had to do.

Ev checked for a pulse and found one on Will's wrist. Thank god he was still alive.

"Will get up, come on Will come back to me."

After a few moments of shaking him, Will opened his eyes.

"Ev…what happened?"

"My god Evelyn he killed Grant."

"Will we have to get out of here, he's going to kill everyone, and we have to save who we can."

"He's won hasn't he Ev?"

Evelyn could feel her heart break as Will said the words. Eiri was too strong and as much as she wanted to stop him, she couldn't.

"For now Will, for now."

The people still scrambling around her, fleeing for their well-being brought a certain notion of empathy that Evelyn couldn't control. She had to help them because if she couldn't stop him then at least she could maybe damage control his influence. Maybe that's why she was brought to this, maybe in all this suffering Evelyn Towne was the buffer between the destruction of Eiri and the deaths of countless more innocent bystanders.

"Okay Ev how do we do this? He's still out there."

"We do it together and we'll need help."

"If we get to a phone I can call a few people from my old department."

"Steve is also still out there, he can help us too."

"I'm sorry Ev I thought…"

"Don't do that Will, we both tried. He's just too much right now."

~

Eiri felt it. The calm in his bones and the slow of his heartbeat and he knew he'd done it. He'd won. The city's core now lay in rubble and concrete slabs and those who came to oppose him had failed and failed miraculously they had, though he never expected otherwise. Doubted though he was, he never doubted himself and it had come to fruition in the wrath of his might. The city, nay the world would never forget his name. He saw the fallen heroes gathering people with help of their emergency friends and he allowed them to leave. There wasn't a need to take them all out, and then who would witness his rise? He had to leave some to tell the tale of his power, his rage. As he surveyed the remnants of what remained of downtown Edmonton he focused on Stantec Tower, it was the tallest tower downtown. That would be his fortress, his castle, the rock upon which he would build his church. For the first time in a long time Eiri smiled.

~

"He's holed up in what used to be Stantec Tower."

"We know Evelyn we've been tracking him quite extensively."

"So what do we do from here? Are we going to stop him?"

Evelyn had just met Nadia Nicholson and initially she thought her to be another heartless government suit but as they interacted and discussed what to do about Eiri going forward she came to respect her, even admired her a little bit.

"We do have an idea and Evelyn we want you to meet someone."

Evelyn wasn't sure who would be important enough to interrupt this meeting but she couldn't say much since she knew she needed the help if she wanted to take back their city.

"Evelyn this is Elena Solis."

"I'm sorry I don't mean to be ru…"

"I'm Eiri's soulmate and I have his kid."

Evelyn felt a sharp stab in her chest and it almost brought her to tears. This was their way out, this was how they got to him.

"He has a kid?"

"Yes and she's just as strong as he is."

Evelyn watched as a young girl who couldn't be more than ten walked into the room. A mixture of emotions hit Evelyn, a thousand questions flooded her mind but she knew that finally they had some sort of hope.

For the first time in a long time Evelyn smiled.

## The End Of The Book One

Printed in the USA
CPSIA information can be obtained
at www.ICGtesting.com
LVHW090123180524
780603LV00001B/135